ALLY'S WORLD

Crushes, Cliques and the Cool School Trip

"Hey, Ally – there's your mum," Kellie suddenly alerted me. "What's she saying?"

I didn't really want to look too closely at Mum and Ivy and the dogs out there in the crowd, just in case I went stupidly blubby, but then Mum *was* definitely mouthing something to me. I stood up and slid open the tiny panel at the top of the window and shouted, "What?" in her direction.

"Look out for the worms!" she laughed, holding her wavy hair away from her face with one hand.

"OK!" I croaked back with a smile, though I was feeling sadder than ever.

All I wanted to do was stay home and make jokes with my mum about Brownie camp, instead of being stuck in the middle of nowhere with Sandie the Mad Texter, Kyra the Clubber and Feargal the Brain-dead for company.

Urgh...

Was this school trip destined to be the lousiest ever in the entire history of school trips...?

Available in this series:

The Past, the Present and the Loud, Loud Girl
Dates, Double Dates and Big, Big Trouble
Butterflies, Bullies and Bad, Bad Habits
Friends, Freak-Outs and Very Secret Secrets
Boys, Brothers and Jelly-Belly Dancing
Sisters, Super-Creeps and Slushy, Gushy Love Songs
Parties, Predicaments and Undercover Pets
Tattoos, Telltales and Terrible, Terrible Twins
Angels, Arguments and a Furry Merry Christmas
Mates, Mysteries and Pretty Weird Weirdness
Daisy, Dad and the Huge, Small Surprise
Rainbows, Rowan and True, True Romance(?)
Visitors, Vanishings and Va-Va-Va Voom

And look out for:

Hassles, Heart-pings! and Sad, Happy Endings...
A Guided Tour of Ally's World

Find out more about Ally's World at
www.karenmccombie.com

ALLY'S WORLD

CRUSHES, CLIQUES AND THE COOL SCHOOL TRIP

KAREN McCOMBIE

SCHOLASTIC

FOR ANita – the PERSON who said,
"WhY doN't YOU CaLL it 'ALLY'S WORLd'?"

Scholastic Children's Books,
Commonwealth House, 1–19 New Oxford Street,
London WC1A 1NU, UK
A division of Scholastic Ltd
London ~ New York ~ Toronto ~ Sydney ~ Auckland
Mexico City ~ New Delhi ~ Hong Kong

First published in the UK by Scholastic Ltd, 2004

ISBN 0 439 97863 7

Typeset by TW Typesetting, Midsomer Norton, Somerset
Printed and bound by Nørhaven Paperback A/S, Denmark

10 9 8 7 6 5 4 3 2 1

Contents

PROLOGUE

Dear Mum,
Do you know something? Until I was 12, I honestly believed that there was such a thing as a Brownie badge for Screaming.

Well, Brownies have badges for all sorts, don't they? There's a Brownie badge for Bell-ringing, a Brownie badge for Circus Skills, a Brownie badge for Knitting (as well as one for Knotting), and even a Brownie badge for Hamster Stroking, so why shouldn't there be a Brownie badge for Screaming?

OK, so I made up the badge for Hamster Stroking, but it wasn't till I met Sandie (who had – unlike me – actually been in the Brownies for more than five minutes*) that I realized you'd made up the Screaming one too. I guess that when you told me all about your very first camping expedition with the Brownies, I was only about seven at the time and very gullible.

Now I'm 13 and a lot (well, a *bit*) less gullible, and although I know the Screaming badge thing wasn't true, what you *did* tell me about that first trip of yours away from home, away from Grandma and Grandad, still makes me laugh. How did your diary entries go again? Wasn't it something like...

MONDAY: Got to camp. Walked for miles. There were big worms in our tent.

TUESDAY: Woke up. Found army of ants crossing my sleeping bag.

WEDNESDAY: Woke up. There were snails all over the inside of our tent.

THURSDAY: Megan James had a frog in her sleeping bag.

FRIDAY: Found slug in my shoe (too late).

Even though you're an animal lover, Mum, I guess that sharing a tent (or worse still, a *sleeping bag*) with a bunch of creepy-crawlies** is taking things a bit too far. No wonder you and your friends all ended up screaming at the top of your nine-year-old lungs.

I think camping and snail-infested tents have gone out of fashion with the Brownies now – they get put up in slime-free hostels where the only disgusting thing is other people's smelly socks littering the floor. When I went on my geography field trip with school, it was a pretty yucky surprise to find out that Kyra's feet were so whiffy.

(Put it this way, I don't think I'll be able to face a packet of cheesy Wotsits again...)

Apart from Kyra's whiffy feet***, there was plenty more stuff to moan about. Maybe we didn't have slugs and snails, but we had something just as creepy, i.e. that bunch of butter-wouldn't-melt-in-their-mouths girls from Westbank School. Thanks to them (mostly****), I got into more trouble than I ever have in my life, without even trying. In fact, do you think they do a Brownie badge in Getting Into Trouble Without Even Trying? 'Cause after last week, I think I *definitely* deserve it.

I know I burbled about my hassles when I got back home, but just in case I was burbling too much to make any sense (well, I *was* in shock – for all sorts of reasons), here's everything you need to know – crushes, cliques and all – about my school trip. (Just flick past the bits about Kyra's feet if you're reading this while you're eating...)

Love you lots,
Ally
(your Love Child No. 3)

* I went twice, but Brownies clashed with *Top of the Pops*, and *Top of the Pops* won.

** Don't let on to Tor that I wrote this – he'll be

very offended and end up making banners that say "Slugs have feelings too!" or something.

*** Maybe if Kyra hadn't worn such stupid shoes on the trip, her feet mightn't have been so whiffy. I mean, who wears platform ankle boots (without socks) when you're hiking around hillsides all day? (Kyra Stupid Davies, *that's* who.)

**** Other people who landed me in mega-trouble were Sandie (by accident), Kyra (no surprise there), and ... well, you're just going to have to read on to find out who else!

Chapter 1

BEWARE: MOANING AND COOING AHEAD...

Uh-oh. Chloe was having a strop.

"It's just so *totally* unfair!"

Breaktimes on Fridays are usually great – it's when me and my mates mooch around the corridors talking about the sheer wonderfulness of having a whole school-free weekend in front of us. But breaktime this Friday morning wasn't working out like that. Chloe wasn't a happy bunny and was letting the rest of us know it.

"Why do *you* lot get to have all the fun?" she moaned, ferociously scrunching up the packet of Hula Hoops in her hands (empty, thankfully). "I don't see why *we* can't go on the geography field trip!"

The "you lot" she was talking about was me, Sandie, Kyra and Kellie. The "we" included Chloe (natch), Jen and Salma.

"Um ... maybe it's because none of you are planning on doing GCSE geography?" I suggested, grinning at her.

Straight away, I wondered if teasing Chloe was a smart thing to do; she can be kind of growly sometimes, and this looked like one of those times. What I'd said was true, but from the dirty look Chloe was chucking my way, it didn't seem like she was in the mood for any unwanted dollops of truth.

"But why should the rest of us be stuck at school working for the whole week, Ally, when you're all on this brilliant skive?!" she growled in my direction.

"It's hardly going to be a skive, Chloe!" Kellie butted in, saving me from having to defend myself. "They're going to make us do *tonnes* of project work, *and* go hiking around for days at a time doing it!"

"We're not going to have to go *hiking*, are we?" Kyra frowned at Kellie, apparently in deep shock. The word "hiking" to Kyra was obviously as terrifying as "sensible" or "responsible" in her book.

"Kyra, the clue is in the name; why do you think it's called a 'field' trip?" I pointed out. God, what was she like? Did she think the geography department was going to send us all the way to some big residential school in the middle of the countryside and just expect us to casually flip through an atlas or [illegible]ily whirl a globe around, in-between lounging [illegible]s watching daytime TV?

"But I thought this was a geography trip, not some outward-bound course!" Kyra protested. "I don't have *hiking* clothes!"

Well, that didn't surprise me. I mean, she hardly had a school *uniform*, and that was compulsory. Maybe her blazer and (slack-knotted) tie were regulation, but that stripy, fitted cheesecloth shirt certainly wasn't, and her skirt might have been navy, but it was also denim and had a hem that was nearer her belly button than her knees. It was lucky for Kyra that our old year head, Mrs Fisher (Fish-Face to her non-friends, and there were *plenty* of those), didn't work at Palace Gates School any more. That woman had an uncanny radar for any breaches of school rules, and she'd have had Kyra dragged into her room for a lecture before Kyra and her minuscule mini got a chance to sashay more than five steps along the corridor first thing this morning.

"Well, if *you* don't want to go, *I'll* easily take your place!" Chloe told Kyra, making a sarky dig along the lines of Kyra not knowing her luck.

"I didn't say I *didn't* want to go – I just said nobody better expect me to go abseiling down cliff faces or make camps out of leaves and twigs or anything!"

Ah, there's nothing like a little exaggeration, and

Kyra Davies was an expert at that. She didn't just make a mountain out of a molehill, she could make an entire mountain *range*, with a volcano thrown in for luck. And to think, from Monday I was about to spend a whole week with her, 24 hours a day, with no escape. Was it too late to pull out?

"Kyra! I didn't make out that it was some sort of survival course!" Kellie jumped in. "What I *said* was that there'll be a lot of walking, that's all!"

"Wish *I* could spend the day just walking around, instead of doing double maths or whatever," Chloe moped some more.

I noticed that while Chloe might have been huffing big-time about missing out on the "delights" of the geography trip, Jen and Salma didn't seem in the least bit bothered. In fact, while Chloe moaned on (and Kellie and Kyra bickered), Salma stood idly flicking through her magazine, totally absorbed in which celebrity was in need of a visit from the fashion police this week. Jen didn't seem that fussed about the present conversation either, and was sidling up to Sandie, noseying at what she was scribbling in the back of her pink folder.

"What's that then, Sandie?" I heard Jen ask her, then I sidled over myself, since whatever it was that Sandie was up to was bound to be more interesting than listening to the rubbish Kyra and Chloe were currently babbling.

"Yeah, what is it?" I quizzed my best friend, parking my bum alongside hers on one of the corridor's chunky old-fashioned radiators.

"I'm just writing a letter to Billy," Sandie smiled shyly. "You know, a sort of miss-you-already letter. I'm trying to get it right, then I'll post it tomorrow so he gets it on Monday, once we've left on the coach!"

Urgh.

I know I'm going to come across like I'm as romantic as a dead haddock here, but one quick look at Sandie's miss-you-already letter and I felt my face muscles twang into "yuck!" mode. As soon as I realized I was doing it, I forced my muscles to *un*twang themselves, so Sandie didn't spot how horrified I looked. But I mean, did she really, *really* have to write it on a piece of Brambly Hedge notepaper? I might have thought that was cute when I was five or something, but she was *seriously* sending this to a 13-year-old boy, for goodness' sake. Did she think Billy was going to go "Awww...!" and melt when he pulled that out of the envelope? I'm sorry, but I'd known Billy a lot longer than Sandie had at that point and I was pretty sure that one look at all those cutesy woodland creatures and he was going to crack up laughing. Or barf. Or both. (Yuck! What a horrible thought...)

And as for her nickname for him...

"'*Dear Baby Bear*...'" Jen began to read aloud. "I didn't know you called him that, Sandie! That's *so* cute! And all those little hearts you've drawn around the 'Baby Bear' – so sweet!"

Yeah, sweet like someone's forced you to eat a bag of sugar in three seconds flat as some kind of perverse *torture*.

"Lemme see!" Salma cooed, slapping the shiny pages of her magazine shut and coming over for a gawp at Sandie's letter. "Oh, I *love* the notepaper! That little hegdehog is *adorable*!"

That was it: my friends were all certifiably mad. They were either moaning, whingeing or arguing (Chloe, Kyra, Kellie), or they had jelly and custard for brains, cooing over stuff that was so icky I couldn't stand it.

"What's going on?" smiled Kellie, defecting from the moaning, whingeing arguers, and turning her attention to our huddle around Sandie.

"She's writing a miss-you-already letter to Billy!" Jen filled her in.

"Ooh, that's *soooo* romantic!" Kellie gushed, hugging her bag to her chest. "Go and read it out, Sand!"

Oh, please, no... What if someone in the corridor overheard? They'd think we *all* had jelly and custard for brains! But I knew it would never happen – I usually feel sorry for Sandie, she's so tangled up in shyness, but today I was quite pleased that being shy was such a major part of her personality. There was no *way* she would—

"OK!" Sandie giggled self-consciously. "*Dear Baby Bear –*"

"Shh, you two!" Kellie hushed the still-bickering Kyra and Chloe. "Listen to this!"

"*– being apart from you is going to be the hardest thing I've ever done. I don't know how I'm going to stop myself from* – ohhhh!"

I might have been clenching my teeth together while I was listening to this, and wishing with all my might that something would make it stop (a sudden meteor crashing through the school roof, maybe?) but I hadn't expected to see the Brambly Hedge notepaper vanishing from between Sandie's fingers as if by magic.

Actually, it wasn't by magic at all – it was yanked out of her hand by a smirking Baz Meat-head, who was now bolting over to his gang, which consisted of various other meat-heads, i.e. Mikey D, Mikey F, Ishmail and (uh-oh) Feargal O'Leary.

Feargal O'Leary... I'd done an excellent job of

ignoring him and more-or-less blanking his mates since we'd been back at school. Yeah, so we'd hung out with Feargal and co for about two seconds during the holidays (that night we ran into them at the fairground, and they came back to Kyra's and helped wreck the place), but it was far too embarrassing to talk to them now. Mainly because me and Feargal had ended up almost-but-not-quite-going-out with each other.

Bleurghhh... I was doing an all-over body cringe at the very thought. There's just something about exes, isn't there? I mean, no matter how microscopically small your so-called relationship was, it's still a trauma to see them anywhere in public ever again. It's like with me and Feargal, I'm so mortified whenever I see him that I'd rather hide in the loos for three hours and get detention than pass him in the corridor.

"Dear Baby Bear," Feargal suddenly started to read aloud – *very* aloud – once Baz had shoved Sandie's note into his hand. *"Being apart from you is going to be the hardest thing I've ever done. I don't know how I'm going to stop myself from crying into my pillow every night. I've still got the white chocolate mouse you gave me and I'm going to take it with me and keep it under my pillow so I dream about you* – Oi!"

Like I say, get Chloe in a growly mood and you're in trouble. And Kyra is frankly *always* pretty scary. When the two of them launched a rescue mission for Sandie's letter, you should've seen how fast Feargal and his cronies ran...

"Oh, Ally! I'm so glad we're going away next week now!" Sandie whispered, as everyone settled down at their desks, squeaking and screeching their chairs across the blue lino floor. In her hands, she gently folded her much-crushed Brambly Hedge notepaper and slipped it gently into the side pocket of her bag.

"But I thought you said you'd miss Billy too much!"

"I will!" she shrugged, her cheeks still fluorescent pink after her corridor humiliation at the hands of Feargal O'Leary and that lot. "But I'm just so ashamed, the way *everyone* at school heard Feargal read out my letter in that stupid voice – I'll never be able to face any of them again!"

Sandie was obviously, understandably upset, so it wasn't a good time, I didn't suppose, to point out the fact that not everyone in school was packed into the corridor, and that maybe it wasn't *just* the stupid voice that Feargal put on that made the letter so cringeworthy. I mean, that thing about sleeping with the chocolate mouse under her pillow – didn't she realize she was going to wake up with melted *goo* on her face in the morning?

I didn't mean to be horrible, though – it really was totally evil of Feargal O'Leary and his meat-head mates to shame Sandie so badly. What was it with those lads, always looking for trouble all the time? And if they weren't looking for trouble they were trying to look cool, wearing the hoods of their tops in the upright position at all times.

"Wasn't it brilliant the way Kyra yanked Feargal's hood right down over his face and held it there?" I reminded Sandie, hoping the memory of Kyra and Chloe's rescue mission would cheer her up.

Sandie didn't get a chance to answer – our geography teacher, Mrs Kilkenny, was shushing us all from the front of the class.

"Everyone looking forward to next week's trip?" she smiled brightly.

(Dad says that teachers tend to think of school trips as one long, ulcer-inducing nightmare, so maybe Mrs Kilkenny was grinning because she knew she wasn't coming with us. Honestly, using the excuse that she was eight months' pregnant, just to get out of a school trip...)

Everyone nodded or mumbled yes, as Mrs Kilkenny handed out sheets of paper to people in the front row and asked them to pass them back.

"This is a final itinerary for you, and for your parents, plus some last-minute information about the coach pick-up on Monday morning," she informed us.

Kellie and Kyra, sitting directly in front of us, swivelled round to pass us our info sheets – Kellie with a smile and Kyra with a wink (she was still feeling all fired up and invincible after taking on Feargal and co).

"Thanks," I mumbled, taking a stapled together bundle and passing the rest to Warren Murphy behind me.

"I'm sorry I won't be with you all –"

(Yeah, *right*, Mrs Kilkenny!)

"– but the staff at the residential school are apparently all very nice and very experienced. And of course, you'll also have Mr Martinez, who teaches the other geography class."

Up till that point, I hadn't given the other geography class a single thought. To be honest, the last few weeks had been so manic with Mum coming home and Jen running *away* from home that I hadn't given the field trip much brain-space till the last few days.

But now, here was a jumble of names in front of me: an alphabetical list of everyone from both classes who would be heading off to fields and projects and who-knows-what on Monday morning. One caught my eye – Michael Dennison. Who was he, again? I wondered, not immediately recognizing the name, but knowing he had to be in the other class.

Before I had time to place the face, another name jumped out at me like a rabid Rottweiler...

Oh, no.

Now it made sense – I knew Michael Dennison better as Mikey D. (I always thought the "D" stood for "Drongo".)

And there was no mistaking the other name. Not one like Feargal O'Leary.

Help...

GFC (GIRLS' FAREWELL CRISPATHON)

Me and Feargal O'Leary: the romance of the century (not).

In fact, it's possible to describe the whole story of what went on (or not) with us in six short sentences…

1) Feargal O'Leary was one of those tough boys in your year that you avoid so they don't pick on you.

2) Er, I didn't avoid him enough and he picked on me (he nicked my journal off me).

3) It turned out that Feargal O'Leary wasn't as tough as he seemed – i.e. he picked on me 'cause he fancied me.

4) I kind of liked the softie side I saw in him, and nearly ended up going out with him.

5) Till he got all freaked out about Billy, and didn't accept that he was just my mate, and chucked me because he was jealous.

6) And now I avoid him like the plague. At least I'd been able to up till now…

"Wow, I am *so* glad I'm not going on your geography trip!" Chloe sniggered, tugging open a reluctant bag of nachos so hard that they showered all over Kyra's living-room floor with a sudden bang.

I know, I know... Chloe had changed her tune since yesterday, hadn't she? What a difference a day (and a Feargal) can make.

"I can't believe Feargal's going to be there – he's just going to spend the whole week winding me up, isn't he?" Sandie whimpered from the sofa, her big blue eyes peering over the fat, furry cushion she was clutching. The rest of us girls, meanwhile, were on our knees, scrabbling about on the floor for precious nachos (none of us was fussed about the odd bit of fluff).

"We won't let him," I tried to reassure Sandie. To be honest, I wasn't sure *how* we could do that, but I didn't know what else to say.

"Yeah – I'll sort him out if he starts acting up!" said Kyra, taking a vicious, crunching bite out of a nacho as if she was imagining it was Feargal O'Leary's spinal column.

You know, sometimes it's handy having a friend as feisty as Kyra.

And this afternoon was her idea too – normally we had our GVNs (Girls' Video Nights), but yesterday she'd suggested us all getting together for a GFC (Girls' Farewell Crispathon) while her parents were out shopping. She's got cable (while round at my house we've barely got a TV that *works*) so MTV was blaring out in the background while we chatted, gave each other manicures, and ate our way through a Tesco aisle's worth of crisps. (Actually, it was pretty annoying – I hadn't let my "Nearly Nude" nail varnish dry properly and now had bits of Quaver stuck to the ends of my fingers.)

"Anyway, I wouldn't worry about Feargal and Mikey D," mumbled Salma from beneath two curtains of dark, shiny hair as she concentrated on carefully picking up crisps with the pads of her fingers so that her immaculate plum-painted nails *stayed* immaculate (unlike mine). "There's going to be another school there, isn't there? The two of them will probably see that lot as fresh victims and spend all their time winding *them* up."

Salma had a point. I think we all turned to look at Sandie to see if that had made her feel any better. Only she didn't seem to be listening.

"Sandie?" said Kellie, brushing a bundle of skinny black plaits behind her left ear (and smearing a sprinkling of salt across her hair at the same time, I was pleased to notice – at least I wasn't the only scruff-bucket around here).

Sandie still didn't take any notice; she had her

head tilted down, as if she was gazing at the top of the cushion, which – I noticed – she was no longer clutching.

"Sandie?" I said louder than Kellie had, at the same time reaching over and yanking away the cushion.

"What?" she replied, blinking in alarm at us all, as she gazed up from the mobile phone in her hand.

"Didn't you hear what Salma just said?" I asked her, chucking the cushion I'd stolen away from her on to the floor. (Great – now, not only did I have Quaver-encrusted nails, but also grabbing the cushion had made them smudge too. I didn't dare look at the cushion to check for signs of stray nail varnish…)

"I was texting Billy!" Sandie mumbled in defence.

"Hey, I thought you were seeing him tonight!"

That was Kyra, chucking a fluff-covered nacho straight at Sandie's head.

"Yeah, I am!"

Sandie looked confused, both about the point of Kyra's question and why she'd *ping*ed a crisp at her.

"Well, if you're seeing him tonight, why have you spent the *whole* afternoon texting each other?"

Kyra was right – all us girls were meant to be

hanging out together, i.e. not having lovey-dovey text conversations with our boyfriends.

"But—" Sandie started to protest, right before her phone started to ring.

"Bet you 10p it's Billy..." muttered Chloe, with a wicked grin at the rest of us.

"Hello? Oooh – I just texted you!"

"Billy," the rest of us nodded and mouthed at each other.

"Did you?" Sandie twittered on, then noticed we were all laughing at her. "Awwww... But listen, hold on a minute..."

With a quick "s'cuse!", Sandie untangled her crossed legs, bounded off the sofa and out into the hall, where she could carry on her (cooing) conversation in private.

"Y'know," smiled Kellie, watching the door as Sandie pulled it closed behind her, "since she's been going out with Billy, she's been a lot more ... I dunno ... what's the word?"

"Annoying?" suggested Kyra, right before we all gasped and chucked a hail of crisps at her. (Which was a bit hypocritical of me since I kind of agreed with Kyra.)

"I *was* going to say she's a lot more *confident*," Kellie said pointedly to Kyra. "She seems a lot less shy than she used to be."

We'd all noticed this before, me especially, since I'd known her the longest. Sandie had always seemed like the human equivalent of a dormouse: cute, sweet and timid. Now, having a boyfriend had definitely given her some extra added confidence. It wasn't like she'd turned into a tiger overnight – more like a slightly assertive chipmunk – but the change was good to see. Well, *nearly* everything about the change…

"Confident?!" snickered Kyra, brushing bits of crisp out of her ponytail. "What are you on about? She's had a brain like mushy peas since they've been going out!"

Hmm, I kept my mouth shut but silently found myself agreeing with Kyra again.

"And I tell you something *else*," said Kyra, bold as ever and unfazed by the idea of getting more crisps chucked her way. "If Sandie's going to spend the whole of this stupid trip *pining* for Billy, it's going to be un-blimmin'-bearable!"

Too blimmin' right…

Chapter 3

HELLO? ANYONE LISTENING?!

Speaking of pining…

Sitting beside me on the park bench was a crumpled pile of clothes and misery that looked vaguely like my best boy mate. And his dog.

"*Yappity-yappity-yappity-yap-yap-yap!*"

"It's just … shut up, Precious! It's just that she's going away all week, Ally, and she's going to have this *brilliant* time and she won't think about me at *all*!"

Sigh.

"Billy, when we were all walking up here to meet you, what were you doing?" I tried reminding him, over the noise of his daft-as-a-fish dog.

When me, Tor, Ivy and our mutts trudged (and skipped, and lolloped) up the steep hill towards Billy, he'd been so engrossed he hadn't even heard me calling out to him ("Oi! Plonker!").

"Um … just sitting on the bench? Waiting?" he suggested, looking instantly dopier than our dog Rolf (and believe me, that's *well* dopey).

"*And*?" I pushed him a little harder, tempted to grab the mobile from his hand and gently thwack it against the side of his head as a bit of a clue.

"And?" he blinked back at me, from underneath the brim of his baseball cap.

"*I* know! *I* know!" Tor butted in enthusiastically, like he was in his primary class instead of standing by a bench beside Alexandra Palace. "Billy was reading his phone!"

Normally, it's just me and the dogs who come up on these Sunday morning catch-ups in the park with Billy and his pootly poodle Precious. But 'cause I was heading off on the geography trip first thing tomorrow, my seven-year-old brother Tor had decided to trail my every move today. And wherever Tor goes, Ivy goes, like a little pink-tinted shadow. I'd thought that the minute I met up with Billy on our bench at the top of the hill, my kid brother and sister would be zooming off across the grass, playing lick-chase with Rolf, Winslet, Ben and Precious, but the sight of a miserable Billy had been too intriguing for them. In fact, the last few minutes they'd stood silently staring at Billy as if he was some bearded lady at one of those spooky freak shows they used to have back in old-time Victorian days.

"Exactly!" I nodded at Tor's explanation, then

turned back to Billy. "You were looking at a text that Sandie had just sent you. You told me just now that it was the *third* one she's sent you this morning, and you only *saw* her last night. So she's hardly going to forget you, is she?!"

"I dunno!" sighed Billy, thunking his face dramatically into his hands, as if he'd just heard that Sandie's family were packing up and emigrating to Mars first thing in the morning.

I clocked Ivy pulling a puzzled face, her three-and-a-half-year-old brain trying to figure out what exactly was bugging Billy.

"Ally, why is this boy sad?" she suddenly blurted out, extending her arm and sticking one short, chubby finger *right* into Billy's cheek. (Billy jerked, but chose not to let a small fat finger interfere with his forlorn state.)

"This *boy*," I began to reply to Ivy, trying not to laugh (it cracked me up the way she couldn't remember any of our friends' names), "is sad because –"

I was about to waffle on about Billy and Sandie and next week's trip, but then I decided that Billy's problem was such a *non*-problem that it wasn't worth the explanation.

"– because he's a berk," I said instead, patting Billy on the back at the same time.

"I am not!" Billy blustered, lifting his head up suddenly and frowning his eyebrows together in my direction, like two fair, hairy caterpillars colliding on his forehead. "There's that whole other school going on that trip! What if Sandie meets someone else?"

"See?" I giggled at him. "You *are* a berk, Billy! And you're a *jealous* berk! You thought the *exact* same thing when the French exchange students were here – you were sure Sandie was going to grab a French phrase book and run off with one of them. And did it happen?"

Billy wrinkled his nose a little sheepishly and said nothing.

"Well, did it?" I pushed him, determined to make him see how dumb he was being.

"*Yappity-yappity-yappity-yap-yap-yap!*"

"Igissnot…" Billy mumbled, pulling his baseball cap down over his face till it practically hid his nose.

"Sorry – what was that?" I asked him pointedly, while yanking the peak of his cap back up with one hand and clamping the other around Precious's yapping doggy mouth to shut him up for five seconds.

"I *said*, I guess *not*," Billy mumbled begrudgingly, while Precious bounced up and down on his four white diddy feet, trying to wriggle free. (Our three flopped-out, panting dogs watched this with great interest. You know, if she hadn't been a dog, I could've sworn Winslet was sniggering.)

Poor Billy – he'd got himself in a right pickle over nothing, and now he looked a bit embarrassed, and also slightly freaked out at Tor and Ivy still standing there ogling him like a pair of aliens trying to comprehend some primitive life form on earth.

"Tor, do you want to take the dogs off to play?" I suggested, nodding my head down at Precious in particular.

But Ivy got there first.

"Doggy want to play?" said Ivy, lifting Precious's back legs off the ground. Now I felt sorry for Precious (as well as his owner) – it's not too dignified to find yourself hoisted in the air by your back legs while someone else is holding you by the nose. So I let go *my* end – and immediately regretted it.

"*Yappity-yappity-yappity-yap-yap-yap!*"

"Got 'im!" said Tor brightly, wrapping his arms around Precious's chest and leading Ivy and the other dogs off across the grass, like a small Pied Piper.

"Anyway, Billy, you've got nothing to worry about when it comes to this trip – it's *me* that's got the problem," I started to tell him, as we watched the procession of pooches trotting after Tor, with Ivy in her pink dungarees taking up the rear, holding on to Ben's golden tail. "Feargal O'Leary's coming too."

"Yeah, Sandie said," he nodded.

"I mean, how embarrassing is that going to be?"

"Yeah."

Billy carried on nodding, his eyes focussed on Tor, who seemed to be sharing a bag of wine gums with Ivy and the dogs. (Good – that might weld Precious's teeth together and shut him up for a bit.)

"It's all right avoiding Feargal at school," I chattered on, " 'cause he isn't in any of my classes and there's always zillions of people milling around in the buildings anyway."

"Mmm."

"But how am I going to be able to stay clear of him in some little residential school?"

"Mmm."

"What if I get put in a team or a group with him or something?"

"Uh-huh."

"How awful would that be?"

"Mmm."

"And you're not even listening to me, are you?"

"Mmm."

"I can see your hand moving from here – you're texting Sandie, aren't you?"

"Uh-huh ... erm, what?" Billy blurted in a panic, now his one-tracked mind had tuned into that magical name. (*Sandeeeeeee*...)

"Give it here!" I grumbled, stretching across him and grabbing the mobile out of his hand. "Hey – check out the mess you've made of this message. Serves you right for trying to type with your thumb and without looking. I mean, how's Sandie meant to know what '*ill pgone u laser*' means?"

At least Billy had the decency to blush madly as he wrestled me for his mobile.

"It's supposed to be '*I'll phone u later*'," he burbled, as I leapt off the bench, and stood in front of him, his mobile now clasped between both my hands, behind my back.

"Don't you know it's rude to have a conversation with someone and not even listen to them, Billy?"

For a second, my oldest, dumbest mate seemed to mull that thought over, biting his lip and grimacing. And then I realized that he *still* hadn't been listening to a word I'd been saying...

"Ally, *promise* me you'll look out for Sandie when you're away!" he suddenly bleated. "Please!"

Before I got the chance to tell him he was as

annoying as diarrhoea, the Nokia in my hand gave out a chirruping text tweet.

"No guesses who *that'll* be," I sighed, chucking the mobile at Billy and not even sticking around to hear him tell me it was from Sandie. I was off to have fun with Tor, Ivy and the dogs, instead of sitting on the bench, talking to myself while Billy and Sandie told each other they'd miss each other for the 75th time via text.

As for looking out for Sandie during the school trip; well, the only thing I'd have to look out for was that she didn't dislocate her finger from all the text messaging she was bound to be doing...

Chapter 4

HAVE I LEFT ALREADY AND NOT NOTICED?

Last night, I dreamt that I pulled open the zip of my bag once we arrived at the residential school, and my sister Rowan jumped out of it yelling, "Ta-*naaaa*!".

As if I don't see enough of her…

"Oh! Hi, Ally!" Ro blinked at me, all confused like I'd walked in her room without knocking or something.

Ahem. Whose room was it exactly?

But let's back up here for a second. It had been a long, slow, *tiring* walk from the park just now: Rolf, Winslet and Ben had insisted on sniffing every lamp post and tree on the way (putting their doggy brakes on and staying absolutely *put* if I tried to drag them away); Ivy had decided to play a game of stopping and blowing kisses to any flowers she saw in every garden we passed (till it tired her out and I had to carry her home); and Tor had quizzed me non-stop on the wildlife I might expect to see on my geography trip ("Do you think you'll see a fox? What about a beetle? Or a cow? Or a deer? Or a vole? Or a…").

And then, after I finally managed to carry or drag all the smaller members of my family home, all I really wanted to do was go straight up to my room, shut the door and quietly spend some quality time deciding on which trainers in my collection to pack for tomorrow. But I couldn't do that because: a) Grandma and Stanley were round and wanted to chat for a while (normally nice, but I really just wanted to go upstairs and be on my own for a bit); b) I still didn't have a bedroom door to shut (thanks for not getting round to fixing it, Dad); and c) my room had been turned into a sewing workshop when I wasn't looking. What an interesting surprise!

"Er … what are you doing?" I asked Rowan, while staring down at the place where my bedroom floor should be, and seeing a sea of purple fuzz.

"Isn't it gorgeous?" Rowan beamed, kneeling at the edge of the purple fuzz, and pulling out a bundle of folded, printed tissue paper from an envelope.

"Uh … it's OK," I shrugged. "But like I say, what are you doing?"

"Well, I bought this material yesterday dead cheap in a sale," Rowan began to twitter enthusiastically, as she set to work unfolding the tissue paper and sent all her Indian bangles jangling. "And then Von's mum lent me this brilliant sewing pattern. See?"

The envelope that she flung at me fluttered into my hands. The photo on the cover was of a smiling woman, posing in an ankle-length winter coat, made out of some plain black material. If Rowan was going to make up this exact same coat in that fuzzy stuff, there'd end up being reports in the local paper of purple yeti sightings in Crouch End...

"Yeah, so you're making a coat," I nodded, feeling the slink of a cat rubbing itself against my legs. "But why are you making a coat in *my* room?"

A cat that wasn't Colin detached itself from my legs and tippy-toed its way on to the purple fuzziness, where it stopped in the middle and went into purring, padding overdrive.

"There's more room to spread stuff out up here," Rowan smiled blithely. "You know how cluttered my room is. I'm going to set up the sewing machine on your desk and..."

Yes, I *did* know how cluttered Rowan's room was, and I *also* knew it was twice the size of my little attic bedroom. So I might know that stuff, but it still didn't make any sense, a fact that suddenly dawned on Rowan.

"I didn't think you'd mind, Ally." She smiled

apologetically, as she stretched over and tried to scoop the cat that wasn't Colin off the purple fuzz. "'Cause you'll be away and everything."

"Oops – have I gone already and not noticed?" I asked, with just a sprinkle of sarkiness. "Funny ... I thought this was only Sunday, and I wasn't actually leaving till tomorrow. Silly me!"

"No – it *is* Sunday! It's just that I got so excited I couldn't wait to –"

"– even check with me first?" I suggested.

I never normally get ratty with Rowan – she's too much of an airhead to get properly annoyed with (unless you're our big sister Linn, of course). But right now, I was mad at her for jumping the gun and taking over my room before I'd even packed my *toothbrush*. So mad that I didn't even manage to crack a smile when I saw the whole of her sheet of purple fuzz lift straight off the floor, firmly attached to four sets of claws, when she tried to get the cat that wasn't Colin off her future coat.

"Sorry, Ally! But now I've got it all laid out, is it OK if I do the pinning and cutting?"

"Whatever, I'll pack later..." I grumbled, turning to go and nearly tripping over Rolf, who'd appeared from nowhere and settled down for a stretched-out snooze across the whole width of the attic hallway.

For a second I looked at Linn's closed bedroom door with envy. I mean, not only did she have a *door*, but she kept it shut *and* kept everyone too scared to dare to go in there and infect her perfect, peaceful hideaway with their noisiness and messiness. Eek! That had to stop – I didn't want to find myself turning into a 13-year-old, neat-freak, nit-picking Linn mini-me...

"I won't be long! Just an hour! Or maybe two!" Rowan's voice trailed behind me as I stomped downstairs, stepping over another cat that wasn't Colin, a pink teddy, a cat that *was* Colin, some bits of a jigsaw and a broken biscuit on the attic stairs alone.

"Y'know, maybe Linn's right about this place being a madhouse," I mumbled to myself, as Tor and Ivy's shrieks and yells from downstairs competed for ear-space with Mum and Dad and Grandma laughing at some joke Stanley had just told them, while the radio blared out unlistened to in the kitchen. "*You* don't like all this noise either, do you, babes?"

That was me talking to Winslet, who I'd just spotted skulking commando-style (i.e. tummy close to the ground – not hard to do when your legs are practically a centimetre long) into Mum and Dad's room.

I went to follow her in, far enough to pat her scruffy, furry head, when I spotted something strangely familiar in her jaws. But in a flash, Winslet spotted me eyeing up her new-found "treasure", and shot straight under the bed with it.

And so five minutes later, that's where Grandma found me; on the floor of Mum and Dad's room, using an old hockey stick to try and hook my brand new bra out of Winslet's mouth.

"What are you doing, Ally, dear?" I heard Grandma ask, and managed to batter my head against the wooden bed frame as I tried to turn and answer her.

"I bought some new underwear for going away, and Winslet's nicked it," I explained.

"Well, you can rescue that in a second, dear. Come up here and chat to me for a moment."

Reluctantly, I scrambled to my feet and sat down on the edge of the orange duvet, where Grandma was patting a place for me. Don't get me wrong, it wasn't that I was reluctant to chat to Grandma – I was just stressing out about Winslet chewing my brand new bra, and wondering if I was going to have time to rescue it, wash the drool off it and get it dry in time for tomorrow morning…

"Big scary old day, tomorrow, isn't it?" she

smiled, gazing intently at me through her oval, gold-rimmed specs.

How does she know about Feargal coming on the trip? I thought to myself, wondering if Grandma had suddenly developed a previously unknown psychic streak. Course, maybe Mum or Dad had told her – I'd moaned to them about it on Friday night. ("Ignore him, Ally Pally," Dad had advised me. "No, just smile at him if he tries to wind you up – that always confuses people when they're trying to be mean!" Mum had said.)

"I guess so," I shrugged. Was Grandma going to give me her own chunk of advice about how to deal with Feargal? "Tell him you've got a three-year-old sister who's more mature than him!"; I bet that's the sort of thing she'd suggest...

And then I got confused – was that a hint of a glimmer of some watery-ness glinting in my usually matter-of-fact gran's eyes? No! It couldn't be, could it? And why would she be watery-eyed over Feargal being on the geography trip, however uncomfortable that was going to be for me?

"First time away from home ... away from your family..." she said in a soft, gentle, grandmothery way (i.e. not the way she speaks at *all*). "It must feel a bit strange, does it, Ally, dear?"

Well, no it didn't. Not till right then, when she

went a bit mushy around the edges and I suddenly realized that it *was* the first time I was going to be away from my family. Overnight sleepovers a few streets away didn't count; this week I was going to be far, far away from Crouch End, all on my own (virtually), while my parents and sisters and brothers and pets were all cosy together, laughing and chatting in our lovely, big, messy house.

Without *me*…

"Now, now – no point getting all sentimental about it," said Grandma, in a more practical, Grandma-style voice, as soon as she spotted my eyes welling up.

Hey – she'd started it!

"Anyway, I know you don't have a mobile, but just so you can stay in touch with your mum and dad, here's a special phone card. You just key in this code number here before you dial…" Grandma explained, handing me a plastic card and a piece of paper with some instructions printed neatly on it in her handwriting, "…and then all your calls will be billed to my account. All right?"

"Yes. Thank you, Grandma," I smiled a wobbly, grateful smile at her.

"And if you've got time, you can always give your old gran a buzz while you're away too."

"Course I will! Every night!" I assured her

quickly, feeling a tear teeter on the edge of one eye.

"Oh, don't be silly, Ally! You'll be far too busy having fun to go phoning *me* every night!" she smiled, handing me an unrumpled paper tissue from her trouser pocket. How does she do that? Tissues always end up in fluff-covered jumbles in *my* pockets – that's if they haven't *disintegrated* first.

"But I will, Grandma, promise!" I muttered, all overcome with a jumble of love for my lovely family who I was going to miss so much...

And then I heard a crunch – the sound of one of the underwired bits in my new bra snapping between two *jaws*, if I wasn't very much mistaken – and I forgot my tears and remembered the hockey stick...

Chapter 5

CAN I PLEASE CHANGE MY MIND AND STAY?

"Bye, bye, Bobbie – see you in a week!"

Sandie appeared to be talking to a bundle of clothes wrapped in several cuddly blankets, all stuffed into a buggy. But on closer inspection you could just about make out a pair of startled blue eyes peering over the top of all the padding.

"Roberta's going to miss her big sister, isn't she?" Sandie's mum smiled down at the baby bundle before tugging a cuddly hat further down on the baby's head so her eyes were nearly covered.

"There's so much padding around that baby that she could crawl out of it all and escape one day and no one would notice," Mum whispered, standing next to me in her long hippy skirt, T-shirt and thin black cardie with the sleeves pushed up.

"Sandie's mum has a thing about catching chills," I explained to Mum. "It's like, if she was the Prime Minister, she'd make it a law that you had to wear vests and gloves all year round," I whispered back, grinning broadly.

It was great having Mum (and Ivy and the dogs) here to see me off on the coach this morning – the only other parents that had come along seemed to be the fretting, fussing type, all doing panicky, last-minute cross-checks of the contents of their kids' bags. And then there was Mum, standing casually with her long, wavy blonde hair blowing in the wind, surrounded by three bouncy dogs, a small bouncy girl dressed entirely in pink, happily cracking jokes and people-watching with me.

"I hope you're going to be warm enough," we heard Sandie's mum say next. "Maybe I should have packed you another fleece..."

Automatically, me and Mum both glanced at Sandie's frighteningly bulging, mega-normous suitcase.

"I don't think there's room for another *sock* in there," Mum mumbled under her breath.

It was true – how much warm stuff had Mrs Walker made Sandie stuff in there? It was as if she'd got in a muddle and got Sandie all kitted out for a bitterly cold mid-January, instead of some pretty nice, early autumn weather. Either that, or she'd read the geography department's info sheet wrong and thought our field trip was to *Siberia* instead of the English countryside.

The big joke was, Sandie probably wouldn't even notice if she left her entire suitcase behind on the pavement – the only important piece of luggage for her was her mobile phone (guess why?).

"Hey, Ally…" I heard Mum say. "That boy by the bus; he's looking over here. That isn't the famous Feargal, is it?"

Cue my stomach pirouetting itself into an instant knot. I wanted to look and check if it *was* Feargal, but at the same time, there was no way I wanted to be caught gawping at him.

"What does he look like?" I asked Mum surreptitiously, as I leant over and scratched the top of Rolf's scruffy head (a good bit of cover, plus Rolf was loving it).

"Let's see … he's black, he's cute-looking, he's pretending to be really bored, and he's got his hood up," Mum informed me. "Oh, and there's a dopey-looking white lad beside him, who's also got his hood up."

"Yeah, that's Feargal," I muttered, while Rolf drooled. "And the other one's Mikey D."

Now Ben wanted in on the head-scratching action and was sitting hip-to-hip with Rolf, smiling a hopeful doggy smile at me. Winslet wasn't bothered, and was merrily sniffing her way around the crowded playground, dragging Ivy by the lead after her.

"You know, I'm sure those two won't bother you girls too much," said Mum, casually putting an arm around my shoulders. "Now that they're away from the rest of their gang, they'll probably be a lot less cocky. Bet they'll be good as gold."

Er, actually I wouldn't like to bet on that, I thought, as I did some stereo doggy head-scratching. But before I could say as much out loud to Mum, another one of *my* little gang turned up.

"Hi, Ally! Hello, Mrs Love!" said Kellie brightly, appearing by our side, and looking like she might just topple backwards under the weight of the big nylon rucksack on her back.

"Hi, Kellie!" I smiled, noticing that she had another bag under her arm, which was stuffed full of more magazines than you'd find in a rack at the hairdressers.

"I love your hair, Kellie," said Mum, lightly touching the tiny turquoise beads at the end of every tiny black plait. "Did you get that done specially for going away?"

"Uh-huh," Kellie nodded, bending down a little so that a curious Ivy – who'd been dragged back in our direction by Winslet and was now stretching up on tiptoes – could get a better look. I reached out automatically to grab at a corner of Kellie's rucksack, just in case she overbalanced. "My cousin Neesha came round yesterday to do it, *and* she lent me her CD Walkman and a whole load of CDs!"

Loads of magazines and CDs ... great! Having Kellie on this trip was going to be like having our own personal entertainment centre.

"Nice flowers!" Ivy suddenly announced, having lost interest in Kellie's braid beads and turned to stare at something *else* that had caught her eye. (Ivy might look and act a lot like Tor, but her addiction to anything pink, or pretty, or both showed that she was lots like her big sis, "yes-I'm-a-glitter-addict!" Rowan...)

The nice flowers that Ivy was referring to were loud, daisy-type blobs on a small plastic holdall that was being carried by someone who was apparently about to go *clubbing*.

"Kyra! What are you wearing?" I asked her straight out, as she strolled her way over to us, in platform ankle boots, a flared mini, and her pink T-shirt with "Boys Suck, Girls Rule" printed on it.

"What?" shrugged Kyra, swinging her bag back and forth. "You've seen this stuff before! It's not new! It's just old stuff, since we'll be roughing it!"

The Queen might have an old crown, and a second-best ballgown, but it doesn't mean she'd stick *that* on for a trip to the countryside. Honestly, the way Kyra's mind worked, there were times when I wondered if she'd ever had a fuse blow in her brain...

"Hey, girls – your teacher's calling for you to get on the coach," Mum interrupted all of a sudden.

Sure enough, there was Mr Martinez, clapping his hands together and trying to get everyone's attention.

I felt Mum's arms curl around me, and a smaller pair of arms circle tightly around my leg. A rough tongue belonging to one of the dogs (hopefully) even started to lick my hand frantically. Instantly I wanted to stay right here with my family (human and furry) instead of clambering on a coach to some unknown destination.

"Go on, hurry," Mum said cheerfully, as she broke away and shooed me towards the coach.

And somehow I had to concentrate really hard on not crying, and stumbled off after Kellie and Kyra and Sandie, who'd managed to wrangle free of her own mum just as Mrs Walker was trying to tuck Sandie's jumper into her jeans "to keep the heat in".

Once we'd dumped our bags for the driver to

pack (the poor guy was going to get a *hernia* after lifting Sandie's case into the luggage compartment), there was a mad scramble for the coach door, as if the thing would run out of seats or something.

"Let's sit at the back!" Kyra said over her shoulder, as she stomped up the metal stairs.

"Let's not – Feargal and Mikey D are already there," Kellie muttered, swirling instead into the very front pair of seats, where Kyra thumped down beside her.

I quickly bagsied the seat on the opposite side of the aisle, and patted the place next to me for Sandie.

"Thanks!" she said brightly, flopping down on to the swirly-patterned seat. "Hey, look – I just got a text from Billy!"

"Uh-huh," I nodded blankly, as the engine rumbled into life and the driver prepared to start off. Between now and the end of the week, how many times was Sandie going to say those same words? It was enough to fry my brain thinking about it...

"God, it's freezing in here!" I heard Kyra grumble. "D'you think they'll stick the heating up?"

"Why don't you put a jumper on?" Kellie suggested.

"A *jumper*? Are you kidding, Kel?!" squawked Kyra. "They are *so* naff!"

Oh, good grief…

"Hey, Ally – there's your mum," Kellie suddenly alerted me. "What's she saying?"

I didn't really want to look too closely at Mum and Ivy and the dogs out there in the crowd, just in case I went stupidly blubby, but then Mum *was* definitely mouthing something to me. I stood up and slid open the tiny panel at the top of the window and shouted, "What?" in her direction.

"Look out for the worms!" she laughed, holding her wavy hair away from her face with one hand.

"OK!" I croaked back with a smile, though I was feeling sadder than ever.

All I wanted to do was stay home and make jokes with my mum about Brownie camp, instead of being stuck in the middle of nowhere with Sandie the Mad Texter, Kyra the Clubber and Feargal the Brain-dead for company.

Urgh…

Was this school trip destined to be the lousiest ever in the entire history of school trips…?

Chapter 6

A ROOM WITH A VIEW (AND A GRUDGE)

So, a quick description of the journey from hell (otherwise known as the coach trip)…

3 – number of hours it took to get to the residential school.

4 – number of times Kyra whined to Mr Martinez about getting the heating on the coach turned up.

4 – number of times Mr Martinez told Kyra not to be silly, it wasn't cold.

0 – number of warm clothes Kyra had brought with her.

17 – number of times Billy texted Sandie.

3 – number of times Marc Simmons was travel-sick.

27 million – number of times Feargal and Mikey D took the mickey out of Marc Simmons for barfing.

49 – number of times Warren Murphy kicked the back of my seat when he was sleeping. (Don't know about you, but I've never heard of "sleep-kicking" before.)

1 – number of times Kellie got everyone to do a

singalong to "The Wheels On The Bus Go Round And Round" for a laugh.

14 – number of rude lyrics that Feargal and Mikey D started singing to "The Wheels On The Bus Go Round And Round".

15 – number of times Mr Martinez had to scream at everyone to "calm down and be *QUIIIEEEETTTTT*!!!"

A trillion – number of times I really, *really* wished I'd stayed home instead of coming on this trip (even if it *did* mean I'd be stuck in maths class right now...)

But the "fun" coach journey was over. We'd arrived (thank goodness).

"He's *cute*!" whispered Kyra, giving me a kick on the ankle (ouch) to emphasize her point.

"And he's a *teacher*!" I whispered back, shocked. Though I shouldn't *really* have been shocked, since it *was* Kyra saying it.

His name was Alan Evans – it was the first thing he'd told us in this welcome meeting. He was young-ish, wore jeans and a washed-out old T-shirt, and had a floppy hairdo a bit like Liam Gallagher used to. He didn't look like someone who ran a residential school to me; he looked more like he'd been on the way to play a gig somewhere and taken a wrong turn.

"So, that's what you'll be doing this week. Anybody got any questions?" said Mr Evans, putting the chalk he'd been using down on the table in front of him. "Yes – you there. What's your question?"

Me and my mates all leant forward to check out who was brave enough to stick their hand in the air. For the last twenty minutes we'd all been sitting here listening to Mr Evans talking, and no one had said so much as a peep. Guess it was 'cause all of us from Palace Gates School were a little wary of all of them from Westbank School, and vice versa. Though there had been *one* constant sound that I could hear while he yakked on – the *click-click-click-click* of Sandie feverishly texting right beside me.

"Well, uh..." began some spiky-haired boy, one of the Westbank lot. "I was just wondering if we get to watch TV, Mr Evans."

Mr Evans let out a laugh, but I could see Mr Martinez and a couple of teachers who'd come from the other school (Miss Moore and Mr Winters) roll their eyes.

"I *was* hoping for a question that had more to do with your projects for this week," grinned Mr Evans. (He had sideburns, I noticed. I wasn't sure if I liked that or not.) "But since you ask, yes, you can watch TV in the evenings. In fact there's a TV room just down the corridor..."

A ripple of "yays!" rumbled around the vast room, plus a couple of grunted "whoo-whoo-whoo!"s that sounded suspiciously like they were the sort of thing Feargal O'Leary and Mikey D would come out with.

"...and you don't have to call me Mr Evans – just call me Alan."

More ripples ran round the room (plus a couple of snorted "fnarr!"s), as everyone squirmed at the idea of calling a teacher by their first name. I guess it was just too weird; it was like answering the phone to your gran and saying, "Yo, sista!" or something.

"OK, so before we get on with this afternoon's work," just-call-me-Alan carried on regardless, "I guess we'd better get you settled. Now, boys, if you could all follow me, I'll take you up to your floor. And if you girls could just talk amongst yourselves for five minutes..."

Us? Talk amongst ourselves? Ooh, I think we could manage that.

"Look! I just got two messages from Billy!" Sandie exclaimed, holding up her phone so we could all read them.

"*'What u doing?'* Wow, that's exciting!" I joked,

but Sandie didn't hear me 'cause she was busy calling up the next message.

"*Goin 2 play Giant Jenga in Hassan's garden after school.*"

Hmm, riveting.

"You going to phone him later, Sand?" Kellie asked.

"Can't – not allowed," Sandie shook her head and stared at Billy's message fondly. "Mum said I'll stay on the phone too long talking, so she said we're only allowed to text, 'cause it'll work out cheaper."

Er, not the amount of texting *Sandie* was planning on doing.

"Nice ... dork ... dork ... OK ... yuck ... *cute* ... dork..."

That was Kyra, giving Sandie's unsensational texts only the faintest glance, while mumbling her verdict on each of the lads shuffling out of the door.

Sandie and Kyra: they both had boys on the brain, in their own irritating ways.

"Just think – what'll happen by the end of the week, Ally?" Kellie whispered to me, staring around at all the remaining girls sitting in the common room. Not that it was very common; Tarbuck House had been a rambling old manor house before it got changed into a residential school. And even though there were dull, grey carpet tiles on the floor and the walls were painted boring white, you could tell by the wooden panelling and the dusty old chandeliers dangling above us that this place had been dead posh once. You could practically *hear* the swish of big, floor-sweeping frocks and tinkle of bells as some snobby lord-type rang for the servants to come and turn the page of his newspaper for him or polish his slippers or whatever.

"I know," I nodded in answer to Kellie's question. "It's funny to think, who'll be mates with who, or who'll fall out with who, I guess!"

In case you were wondering, I'd perked up a bit after the endless (and endlessly annoying) coach trip. For a start, I was pretty impressed with Tarbuck House, and second, I'd just got a ripple of excitement seeing all these new faces and not knowing what the next five days would bring. I mean, over by the window, there was the group of three girls who all looked really smiley and friendly, and one of them had on the exact same T-shirt as me (green with a red star). I know it's mad to think you might be matey with someone just 'cause they've got the same taste in clothes, but then again, why not? Maybe by Friday those three girls would be swapping addresses with me and Kyra and Sandie and Kellie. Who knew?

"Wonder who'll be *snogging* who," murmured Kyra, as the last of the boys – our class's resident know-it-all, sleep-kicking Warren Murphy – shuffled out the door.

You know something? Kyra was *bound* to to be involved in any potential snogging that might happen this week, sure as the sky is blue and pigs are pink...

"Let's have this one! It's really nice!" Sandie called out excitedly, after racing up the corridor ahead of us to check out the furthest away room. (How she'd managed to scurry so fast while she was dragging that mega-normous suitcase of hers I have no idea...)

We were on the second floor of Tarbuck House, tearing around like all the other groups of girls, trying to bagsie the best dorm. All the boys were supposedly "settled" on the first floor, although with all the roaring going on they sounded more like they were at a football match than unpacking their bags. One flight up, on the third floor, there were a couple more girls' rooms – with brilliant views, just-call-me-Alan had said – but so many people had been desperate to nab those that we didn't even bother trying.

"It's right on the corner and there's loads of windows!" Sandie yelled some more, straddling the doorway and waving us to hurry up.

As me, Kyra and Kellie hurried towards her, our bags banging against our shins, someone behind us on the first-floor stair landing let out an irate "Oi!".

"What's that all about?" said Kyra, as we all turned to see what was up.

"That's *our* room! We already bagsied it!" shouted a girl with long fair hair – in the T-shirt that was the double of mine.

Yep, it was one of the three girls I'd thought looked smiley and friendly in the common room a few minutes ago. She and her two mates were absolutely *charging* towards us, like a bunch of raging bulls (with sports holdalls).

For a second, I couldn't figure out who the girl in the matching T-shirt was talking to – there were a lot of people milling about the corridor – but as T-shirt girl and her buddies rushed passed us tight-lipped, it dawned on me that she'd been snarling (yes, *snarling*) at *Sandie*.

"But ... but there're no bags in there!" Sandie stumbled, her blue eyes bulging in shock at the three girls steamrollering in her direction.

Hey ... that was my best friend they were shouting at; no *way* was I going to let them get away with that. And neither were Kyra or Kellie – once we'd got over a moment's worth of shock, we zoomed straight to Sandie's defence.

"Excuse *me*," I began, as I hurried over. "How can you have bagsied that room when we got here first?"

I was asking the fair-haired girl in the matching T-shirt, but also eyeballed her two friends standing either side of her. Both of them, I realized, looked like clones of her, with their longish, straightish, fairish hair and nearly identikit T-shirts and khaki cargo pants. They were even wearing the same style "name" necklaces, not that I was close enough to read what those names were. They were so similar, they looked like Barbie dolls. Make that sour-faced Barbie dolls.

"Danni chucked her cardie on that bed over there, just in case we didn't manage to get one of the rooms upstairs! See?!" snapped the girl in the matching T-shirt to mine, pointing to a purple cardigan that was lying across one corner of one of the four beds that were visible beyond the doorway.

"Wait a minute," Kyra waded in. "You can't go around bagsie-ing *every* room you fancy!"

"Too right!" Kellie added. "It's not *our* fault that you didn't get one of the rooms upstairs!"

"Tough! We can do what we want!" scowled T-shirt girl. "C'mon, Danni ... c'mon, Martha!"

But before Danni and Martha and the girl with the matching T-shirt to mine could barge into the room and claim it, they were stopped by a human shield. Not a very impressive human shield (Sandie's about as fearsome as the Easter bunny), but a human shield with the largest piece of luggage in the Western hemisphere.

"Move it!" demanded the mouthy girl we didn't know the name of yet.

"Move what?" came a voice from behind us. "What's going on here?"

Wow – it was like a secret switch flicked on somewhere. With the approach of a teacher-type, the sour-faced threesome flipped from snarling she-bulls to a pack of adorable Andrex puppies, all wide-eyed and innocent.

"Please sir, me and Danni and Martha really, really wanted this room," whined the girl-with-no-name, who seemed to be the spokeswoman of her nasty little gang. "But *this* girl is trying to stop us having it!"

"This" girl – i.e. Sandie – started to blink madly, as if someone had just shone a torch in her eyes.

"I see," said just-call-me-Alan, glancing around at us all, while flashing a placating smile. "The thing is – sorry, what's your name?"

"Lisa," beamed the girl who now had a name, who now also seemed to have a different personality to the one she had five seconds ago.

"The thing is, Lisa," just-call-me-Alan continued, "this is a four-bed room, so it makes more sense for *this* group of girls to have it."

I think that Sandie breaking into an instant smile at that point wasn't exactly a good move (in fact, it *definitely* wasn't a good move, as we found out later, but more of that, er, later...).

"But I'm just doing a bit of juggling at the moment and I know you and Martha and Danni were interested in the attic rooms – well, one of those is a three-bed, so let's get you up there. OK?"

"OK. Thank you!" Lisa twittered prettily, who along with her two mates started following just-call-me-Alan as he set off along the corridor.

"Don't forget this!" Sandie suddenly called out after them, having jumped over her suitcase and grabbed the girl called Danni's cardie off the bed.

"Thanks!"

"Amazing!" muttered Kyra, as Danni snatched the cardie from Sandie and hurried away. "She managed to make that sound like she meant it, but gave you the filthiest look at the same time, Sand!"

And that wasn't the last of the filthy looks aimed at Sandie. You know, you'd think Lisa's lot would be chuffed, since the third floor was where they'd wanted to be in the first place. But from the evil-eye glare Lisa threw over her shoulder in Sandie's direction as she swanned off, it seemed like she and her mates were planning on holding a grudge against her.

A great big *fat* one, by the look of it…

Chapter 7

TO POP OR TO HOP...

"Check it out!"

"No, thanks."

"Aw, c'mon, Ally! Check it out! How bad is it?"

I ducked away from the skinny, light-brown foot that Kyra was wafting in my face. Friendship's all very well, but you have to draw the line at minging, whiffy feet, don't you?

"Hold on, *I'll* take a look," said Kellie, sensibly holding her nose before she examined the moon-sized blister on Kyra's heel. "God, it's *huge*! D'you want me to pop it for you?"

"No!" squawked Kyra. "That'd be *way* too sore!"

"Well, how do you expect to walk back to Tarbuck House? You can't put your boot back on with *that* blister!" I pointed out.

"Hey, maybe you could *hop* your way back!" Kellie grinned, still holding on to her nose, even though Kyra yanked her leg away and was now gingerly poking at the bulging watery lump under her skin.

"Yeah, maybe I could, if I didn't have a blister coming up on my *other* foot too," Kyra mumbled gloomily. "Whose stupid idea was it to walk this far?"

"Yeah, why can't we all get ferried around in golden carriages pulled by unicorns instead?" I suggested, wide-eyed and teasing. "And maybe we could get some really smart fairies to fly around taking our notes for us too!"

I nearly got a smelly platform boot flung at my head for saying that. But at least Kyra was smiling (instead of moaning) for the first time since we'd been out this afternoon.

"Maybe Alan'll have to give me a piggy-back!" she suggested, wickedly.

What was Kyra Davies like? So cheeky that she made me and Kellie gasp, *that's* how cheeky. Sandie wasn't gasping – *or* listening – she was too busy fiddling with her phone. *Again*.

You know, if this had been a *normal* Monday at 4.10 p.m., I'd probably have been at home, lying on the sofa, with a packet of crisps in one hand, a purring cat on my chest, chilling out and working up the energy to go and do my homework. But *this* Monday at 4.10 p.m., I was sitting on a (dampish) patch of grass on a village green, resting – along with everyone else – after a five-kilometre hike, while dodging Kyra's whiffy foot. At the same time I was also eyeing up the tiny duck pond and wondering how big a splosh Sandie's mobile would make if I threw it in there…

"This is crazy! How come I still can't get a signal?!" Sandie suddenly burst out, frowning miserably at her phone.

"It's the country. *Everything's* rubbish about the country."

Course, maybe Kyra would have liked the country a bit *more* if she hadn't tried walking around it in a pair of lace-up platform boots with no socks. Just a *wild* guess.

But anyway, unlike Kyra, I'd actually quite liked this chunk of countryside we'd walked through. Earlier just-call-me-Alan had split us all into groups of six (me, Sandie, Kyra and Kellie got landed with pukey Marc Simmons and sleep-kicking Warren Murphy), and then he'd led all the groups around the grounds of Tarbuck House, getting us to make notes about trees and landscape and stuff. After that, we'd wandered over some woody hill and along a really pretty riverbank for a while, until we'd arrived at this village. To me, the only things that had been rubbish about this afternoon so far were:

a) putting up with Kyra's non-stop moaning

about how much her feet hurt (she might as well have been wearing *flippers*, her fancy boots were so useless);

b) avoiding Lisa's lot as much as possible (yes, they were *still* flinging dirty looks our way);

and c) listening to Sandie droning on about her lack of phone signal. (Eek! Would Billy pine away and *die* if he didn't get a text message from Sandie for a whole three hours?!)

"Ally..." Sandie suddenly began, in a tentative, please do-me-a-favour way.

"What?" I answered her warily, wondering what was coming next. Usually that kind of "Ally..." from her was followed by something like, "could you just...?" or "would you maybe...?", or something else that guilt-tripped me into helping her out.

"Would you maybe..."

(See? Told you!)

"...go and ask Mr Evans about the phone signal for me?"

"Er, *no*!" I told her, glancing over in the direction of just-call-me-Alan, who was currently chatting to a couple of lads from Westbank just outside the village shop. "Why don't you go and ask him yourself?"

I knew the answer was, "because I'm too shy",

and normally I'd just sigh and then go and do whatever she'd asked me to do anyway, but today I was a bit fed up with her obsession with texting Billy, and practically ignoring the rest of us. It was like having a little ghost trailing behind us, instead of a living, breathing, fun friend. And maybe it would be nicer if she fancied chatting to nice mates like us who'd stood up for her earlier in the Battle for the Bedrooms, instead of being frantic about texting Billy to tell him all about it.

"Yeah, go on, Sand! Go and ask Alan what he thinks. Billy'll be really worried if he hasn't heard from you!" said Kyra, sounding (amazingly!) interested in something else apart from herself for the first time this afternoon. But it seemed to do the trick.

"Um … OK!"

And with that, Sandie – already blushing at the thought of speaking to just-call-me-Alan – scrambled to her feet and brushed some damp, clingy grass blades from the bum of her jeans.

"Good for you!" Kyra nodded encouragingly. "And hey, could you see if they sell plasters in that shop while you're over there?"

Ah, so *that's* why Kyra had been so encouraging; she'd *wanted* something. See, I knew there had to be more to it then just general friendly thoughtfulness. Kyra doesn't *do* just general friendly thoughtfulness for the sake of it – there always has to be a twist.

"Sure." Sandie smiled obliviously, taking the couple of pound coins that Kyra was holding out to her.

"You're terrible, Kyra Davies!" Kellie told her matter-of-factly, as Sandie headed off. "You don't care if she gets hold of Billy or not. You just wanted someone to run your errand for you!"

"Yeah, yeah, *whatever,*" Kyra droned carelessly, as she tugged at the lace of her other boot. "Anyway, how come we're stuck with dweebs like Marc Simmons and Warren Murphy in our group, when that Lisa girl and her mates end up with those two real hunks?"

I knew exactly who she meant. Those two Westbank boys were the ones who just-call-me-Alan was talking to now, and they were definitely seriously cute. But Kyra didn't have to be so horrible about Marc and Warren. It was like trying to compare hopeless mutts like Rolf and Winslet to fancy-pants, award-scooping Afghan hounds at Crufts or something.

"Kyra! Shut up!" I hissed at her, seeing as those very "dweebs" were on the way back over to us, carrying cans of Coke and some Magnums they'd offered to get for us from the shop.

"Yeah, don't be mean, Kyra – those two are all right!"

"Are you *kidding*, Kel?!" Kyra snorted. "Marc's just a big dork who still smells of sick and Warren is the most seriously boring swot in the world!"

Poor Marc and Warren, I thought, as I watched them hover for a second and fumble around giving Sandie her ice-cream and change. They weren't *that* bad; I mean, Marc did *not* still smell of sick, and it wasn't his fault he was so tall and lanky and wore trainers that were the same size as the pedalos up at the Ally Pally boating lake. And yeah, so Warren was super-smart but a bit dull, but so what? I was pretty pleased he was in our group, for two very specific reasons: first, we might actually manage *not* to fail the geography project miserably with him on our side, and second...

"Just be glad we got Warren and Marc," I whispered to Kyra. "We could've been stuck with Feargal O'Leary and Mikey D instead!"

"Well, they might be pretty obnoxious, but then it could've been more of a *laugh* having them in our group."

Was Kyra completely *mad*?! Didn't she

remember what Feargal and co did to Sandie on Friday, or me last term?

But there was no more time to have a go at Kyra, mainly 'cause Marc and Warren were within hearing distance, and also because – as Kellie was pointing out – Sandie was trying to get just-call-me-Alan's attention. By the way, I did say "trying".

"Come on, Sandie!" I mumbled, willing her not to hover behind just-call-me-Alan and hope he'd somehow psychically *know* she was there.

"Look!" Kellie nudged me. "That lad with the spiky hair! He's pointing her out to Alan!"

"That's really nice of him!" I said, watching as just-call-me-Alan turned and smiled at Sandie, who immediately held up her phone and began to nervously babble.

"Ooh, that lad's *definitely* cute!" Kyra practically purred, focussing in on spiky boy.

"Who's definitely cute?"

"None of your business, Warren," said Kyra. "And give me my ice-cream."

"She's talking about Jacob. *Told* you all the girls would fancy him."

That was Marc, talking as he tried to fold his long limbs into an ungainly pile on the ground.

"How do you know his name?" asked Kellie, taking the can that Marc had passed to her.

"Me and Warren – we're sharing a room with him and his mate Nick."

I was listening to what Marc was saying, but still keeping an eye on Sandie. Not only was just-call-me-Alan animatedly chatting to her, but the spiky boy called Jacob and his mate were joining in too. Jacob was even taking a look at Sandie's mobile, frowning as he fiddled about with it.

"Yes, *and* we have to share with Feargal and Mikey D," Warren grumbled, tap-tap-tapping his foot on the grass.

OK, so that grabbed my attention away from Sandie and her phone exploits. Poor Marc and Warren – no wonder Warren was tap-tap-tapping his foot like that. It looked like a nervous reflex type of thing, but if I'd been forced to share a room with Feargal and Mikey D, I think I'd be pretty nervous too.

"Who*ooahhh*!!" Kyra suddenly roared, making us all jump. "Did you *see* that?!"

She was pointing in the direction of Sandie, just-call-me-Alan, and Jacob and his friend. A sudden "accident" seemed to have interrupted Sandie's conversation with the others. A carton of Ribena appeared to have "accidentally" exploded all over Sandie's white T-shirt. The person who was apologizing theatrically for this "accident" was

Lisa, with her two cronies close by her.

"What's she playing at?! She did that on purpose!" Kyra ranted.

Yeah, tell us something we didn't know…

Chapter 8

I'LL SHOW YOU MINE IF YOU SHOW ME YOURS

"Fish pie, chips and beans."

"What else? Did you get a pudding?"

"Yes – chocolate cake."

"Hmm. That's all right, I suppose," Grandma muttered, having done a quick mental calculation about the nutritional value (or not) of the meals at Tarbuck House.

It was funny, but I realized that everyone wanted to know something different about this trip. When I'd phoned home a few minutes ago, Dad had asked all about the school and if the showers were hot enough (hadn't tried them yet), Mum wanted to know about the scenery and if there were enough blankets on the bed (the duvets looked a bit deflated, but OK), Linn had shouted in the background something about whether the toilets were disgusting (no they weren't, but hygiene is something Miss Perfect always worries madly about), Tor had wanted to know if I'd seen a fox yet (no, just some fat wood pigeons) and Ivy had insisted on coming on the phone and then not asking anything at all (after heavy breathing into the phone for a while, Mum had to take it off her). Rowan's question was the most embarrassing; were there any fanciable boys on the trip? Well, I was hardly going to answer that with a trail of saddo non-mobile owners like me standing waiting to make a call in the corridor, was I? Who knew who'd be listening in?

"I'd be happier if there was some fresh fruit or vegetables," Grandma announced, just as my mind was drifting off, wondering what my friends were up to. (It's not that I don't like speaking to Grandma – I do – but fretting about my vitamin C intake wasn't too exciting when it was our first evening of fooling around at Tarbuck House.)

"Well, we get fruit with our packed lunches," I tried to reassure her, as I kept one ear strained to the roar of raised voices and blaring, broken-up sounds coming from the TV room. What was that all about? It was like a shouting match crossed with a football match, crossed with a dollop of some old Spice Girls song or something.

"Well, that's better than nothing, I suppose. Oh, well ... I better let you go, Ally, dear. Thanks for phoning! And that's Stanley saying hello and goodbye!"

I smiled as I heard Stanley – Grandma's husband

– cheerfully bellowing "Hi! Bye!" in the background. And just for a second I felt the faintest, familiar twinge of homesickness, even though I'd been fine when I'd phoned home earlier. It's funny, isn't it? How one word, or smell, or silly "Hi! Bye!" can ruffle up your emotions and make that weird, hard lump pop up instantly in your throat?

"Er ... bye, then, Grandma. Phone you tomorrow!" I said, willing the homesick wibbles away before I turned and let anyone standing in the phone queue spot how pathetically *wet* I was.

What I needed – and fast – was an antidote to the wibbles. And that was to go and check out what noisy weirdness was going on in the TV room. Ten seconds and a quick stomp along the long, carpet-tiled corridor into the huge, once-grand hall and I found out.

"*Give* me the remote!" I heard a snarly squawk, as I stood in the TV room doorway.

"No *way*!" grinned Feargal O'Leary, holding the remote control well away from the one girl on this trip that I'd come to loathe in a very short space of time.

"*Give* it to me!" she shrieked, lungeing at him. "We're watching the Posh Spice documentary! We're *not* watching some stupid football game!"

Just as she tried to grab the remote, with a bunch of girls (including Danni and Martha, of course) egging her on, Feargal tossed the remote in the air, sending it flying in the direction of Mikey D, who caught it to the roars of the other football-loving boys (and a few girls) lounging about on the rest of the chairs.

It may have been quite good fun to see Lisa getting a hard time, but since Feargal wasn't exactly my favourite person in the world, it didn't give me quite as much of a buzz as I might have expected. Plus, with a quick glance around the room, I realized that none of my friends were in here anyway.

"Hey," said a voice behind me. "Looking for your mates?"

I turned round and saw Warren Murphy, just about to head up the grand flight of stairs, with a magazine in his hand.

"Yeah – seen them?"

"They're in the games room," he told me, chucking his thumb over his shoulder, in the direction of another doorway to another big, noisy room.

"Thanks. Where're you going?" I asked, thinking for a second that Warren looked quite like one of Tor's gerbils – small and earnest and always tap-tap-tapping. He was doing it now – tap-tap-tapping the fingers of one hand on the bannister.

"Up to my room. Want to go and read my new computer magazine."

Now he didn't just remind me of a gerbil, but of my sister Linn too. Not that I could imagine her being desperate to flick through the latest issue of *PC User*, but like Warren she appreciated peace and quiet and space away from irritation (i.e. me and Rowan, usually).

"Sure. OK – see you!" I waved to him.

"See you!" he waved back, looking – weirdly – quite chuffed for some reason...

Then out of nowhere, just as I was padding across the hall towards the games room, a word I'd never used popped into my head: "clique". It's like one of those posh words you sometimes read in fancy old books but never ever say in real life, like "whom", or "insomuch", or "whatsoever". But "clique": suddenly that was the right word to use for Lisa's lot. It's like "gang", but it has that edge of clinginess and bitchiness that really kind of summed up those three little witches back in the TV room. Wasn't it weird that when I first saw them this morning I'd half-wondered if they might end up being substitutes for Chloe, Jen and Salma on this trip? Now I was just hoping they'd get bored and lay off Sandie after today, otherwise they were going to really, *really* work all our nerves this week...

"Yesssss!"

Just like the TV room, there was a lot of roaring going on in the games room. The person responsible for this *particular* bit of roaring was currently jumping around the pool table waving a cue around, her flared mini-skirt flapping around just about enough to give everyone a glimpse of her knickers.

"Kyra, one of your plasters is coming off," I told her, pointing to the large Harry Potter plaster that was flapping off the heel of one of her bare feet.

"Don't care!" she yelped, carrying on with her bounding. "Just beat Nick for the second time! *Yessss!"*

I left her and Nick high-fiving and glanced around the rest of the crowded room. There were people playing table-football, another couple of people playing ping-pong, some lad from Westbank juggling the spare ping-pong balls, some bods sitting on the floor just yakking, and then a whole heap of girls and lads crowded on to a row of computers playing various zapping, kill-'em-dead games. Kellie was there, I noticed, sharing a game – and half a seat – with lanky Marc (ooh, *very* cosy!).

Speaking of cosy, sitting perched on the deep window sill was Sandie – and spiky boy Jacob, both comparing phones (again). Sandie seemed to spot me at the exact moment I saw her, and excitedly waved me over.

"Jacob, this is my best friend, Ally! Ally, this is Jacob!" she said brightly, introducing me to her new buddy. Although I'd clocked him outside the village shop this afternoon, I hadn't met him properly then, 'cause just as me and Kyra and Kellie had started running over to help Sandie after the Ribena "accident", *she* broke away from Jacob and everyone, and started running towards *us*.

"Yeah, I noticed you earlier," Jacob smiled at me.

Aaargh! I hadn't even *thought* about fancying him, but the killer combination of a) him being cute-looking, b) him smiling directly at me, and c) him saying he'd "noticed" me earlier automatically pressed a button deep inside my body somewhere that said "BLUSH!".

"Did you?" I squeaked, wishing my cheeks weren't now glow-in-the-dark fiery red.

"Yeah, you've got the same T-shirt on as Lisa Harrison from my school."

Urgh. So he *hadn't* been instantly attracted to my Kate Moss style good looks then (er, probably because I look more like a heap of mouldy moss than Kate Moss). I just happened to remind him of the Queen of the Clique. *Great*...

"Anyway, Jacob was just showing me his phone –"

Oooh! They were playing a game of "I'll show you mine if you show me yours", with mobiles!

"– 'cause now I can't even get a signal *here*, even though I could earlier!" Sandie announced, her fair ponytail swishing as she spoke. "But Jacob's just saying it's maybe the weather conditions and 'cause the network I'm on must be a bit dodgy for reception in this part of the country. But he's on a different network, so..."

I wasn't too interested in different networks and signals and receptions and whatever; I was just trying desperately to *will* my bad case of blushes away and look like a normal person, instead of one who could join a lookalike agency and take bookings for anyone who wanted a giant tomato at their functions.

Also, my mind was trying to take in the fact that I'd never seen Sandie so chatty and bubbly with someone she'd only known for about five minutes. Especially a *boy* someone. Actually, I didn't think I'd seen her that chatty and bubbly *ever*. It was like the time me and my sisters caught our normally pretty silent little brother Tor eating a whole jar of honey as if it was a tub of Petit Filous yoghurt. He was so high with the sugar hit for the whole afternoon that the only time he stopped chattering was when he got breathless from talking while doing non-stop cartwheels.

"Hey, maybe you should go up to the third floor, and see if the reception's better there!" Jacob suddenly suggested.

"D'you think so?" Sandie asked him, her big, blue eyes gazing trustingly at him.

"Yeah, definitely! Let's go try it and see!" Jacob said enthusiastically, slipping off the windowsill.

Er … what exactly was going on here? Sandie and this spiky-haired stranger getting all matey and zooming off somewhere together?

Don't be stupid, I told myself off. *She's getting his help so she can text Billy.*

Sandie *had* told this Jacob boy about Billy, of course. Hadn't she?

I was just making a mental note to ask her about this in private later when a weird chill ran up my spine. Was it some ghost fluttering by? Some irate, long-dead old duchess all grumpy at having her dining room taken over by noisy young ping-pong-playing ruffians like us?

"Hey, it's Lisa!" said Jacob casually. "See she's changed her T-shirt so you're not twins any more!"

I glanced round and understood why I'd felt the hairs on my neck practically stand to attention just now; hovering in the doorway was the Clique.

Seemed like they'd lost the fight for the remote through in the TV room, but by the matching sniffy, sour looks on their faces as they glowered at Jacob, Sandie and me, they didn't much like what was going on in the games room either.

Hmm. Was that *steam* I could practically see coming out of Lisa's ears...?

Chapter 9

MR PENGUIN, THE STOWAWAY

There was something missing.

I wriggled my legs around under the duvet and was amazed at all the space. If this was me at home in my own bed, I'd be sharing it with some combination of assorted pets, as well as Tor and a variety of his soft toys, if he was in the mood to come up and kip in my bed instead of his. (Mind you, he hadn't had any of his nightmares since Mum came back. Had she scared all the night spooks away with her big smiles and happy, out-of-tune humming?)

But I wasn't at home – I was in my bed in the dorm, with a bunch of pillows at my back, and only Mr Penguin for company (Ivy's favourite toy, which seemed to have mysteriously stowed away in my bag), and three of my best friends for company in the other beds. Well, nearly.

"Just leave that, Sandie! It's never going to come out!" said Kyra, gazing up from the toenails she was carefully painting (Kellie's).

"You're right, it's *never* going to come out!" sighed Sandie, standing over by the tiny sink in the corner of the room and holding up her dripping white T-shirt with the big pink splosh and splatter of Ribena all over it.

"You could always dye it when you get home," I suggested, helping myself to a toffee from the bag Kellie had just chucked my way. "That's what Rowan would do. Either that, or she'd just sew a bunch of sequins round the stains and pretend it was some kind of fancy, arty designer top."

Sandie scrunched up her nose at the second suggestion. I didn't blame her – some of my sister's fashion statements were enough to make you question her sanity. (But at least they were always interesting, in a *mental* kind of way...)

"If I put it on the radiator, d'you think it'll dry?" she asked, letting the soggy material dribble all over the lino floor.

"If the radiators were *on*, it might help," said Kyra, with her usual trace of sarkiness. "I think the best thing you could do with that T-shirt is squeeze out all the water..."

Sandie nodded, waiting for the next instruction.

"...then ... see that window?"

Sandie looked at one of the four big windows in our room.

"Well, I'd go over to that window ... and chuck the T-shirt into the bin that's right underneath it!"

Sandie rolled her eyes, realizing she was the butt of the joke again. She'd been teased solidly all evening by Kyra (OK, and by me and Kellie too), about how much attention Jacob had paid her. Like after she'd gone up to the third floor with him (i.e. after the games room encounter when the Clique stomped off to who-knows-where), it had been a non-stop teaseathon, with no holds barred. A choice (cruel) example…

KYRA: "So what's his last name, then?"

SANDIE: "Eriksson. Why?"

KYRA: " 'Sandie Eriksson' ... got a nice ring to it, hasn't it?"

SANDIE: "Kyra, *don't*! He was only being friendly!"

KYRA: "Yeah, did he tell you that *before* or *after* he snogged you?"

SANDIE: "He *didn't* snog me!!"

Poor Sandie – she really was getting it in the neck. And the night wasn't over yet.

"Whatever. Stop acting like Pauline Fowler in *EastEnders* and leave the laundry alone," Kyra told her. "I mean, now lover-boy's got your phone working again, isn't it time to text Billy for the fifty-millionth time today?"

"*Don't* call Jacob my lover-boy!" said Sandie, flicking sprinkles of water off her fingers at Kyra as she flopped on to her bed. "And I haven't texted Billy *that* much today!"

"Oh, yeah?" I laughed. "And how many times is 'not many'?"

A couple of pink spots flared in the middle of Sandie's white cheeks.

"Twenty-three..." she mumbled, scooping up the phone on the end of her bed.

"Oh, no – you're *not* going to make it twenty-four!" grinned Kyra, leaping off her bed so fast to grab Sandie's mobile that Kellie had to grab the bottle of fuchsia pink nail polish before it spilt all over the cover.

"Give it to me!" Sandie whined, suddenly looking like a five year old whose big brother had nicked her security blanket off her. (Course it didn't help that she was wearing her corny *Little Mermaid* pyjamas. I wished someone would spill Ribena on *those*...)

"Nope!" laughed Kyra, sprinting backwards and holding the phone aloft, a bit like I'd seen Feargal doing with the TV remote earlier. "You're not going to get it back till you admit you *quite* fancy Jacob!"

"Will not!" said Sandie, getting steadily pinker.

"Go on! It's not that hard! Hey, we'll all say our top three boys on this trip, OK?"

Now it was my turn to go a little pink around the edges. Kellie might have been blushing at the very idea too, but luckily for her it doesn't show with her dark skin.

"Come on!" Kyra heckled us all, fearless as ever. "OK – I'll start. Number one: Alan, even if he is a teacher; number two: Jacob – and I'm allowed to fancy him, even if he is Sandie's boyfriend –"

"He is *not* my boyfriend!" Sandie yelped, half angrily, half trying not to smile. (When Kyra gets like this it's like being tickled by someone who won't stop even when you beg them to.)

"– and number three," Kyra carried on regardless, "is Jacob's mate Nick. Very cute. OK, Ally – it's your turn."

"Um ... Jacob, I guess," I shrugged apologetically, though I don't know why. I mean, he really *wasn't* Sandie's boyfriend. "Then Nick, and then ... then Alan."

Well, he *was* a teacher, but I guess Kyra was right; he was allowed on the list.

"Me next! Me next!" Kellie called out. "I think I like Nick best, then Mr Evans – Alan, I mean, and then Jacob."

"Wow – how boring! We all like the same guys!"

Kyra grinned. "So come on, Sandie, it's no big deal. Who's in *your* top three?"

"Same as you lot, I guess," said Sandie, holding her hand out hopefully for her phone.

"Ah, no..." Kyra smiled, stepping back. "You have to tell us which order. It's Jacob first, isn't it, isn't it?"

Sandie bit her lip for a second, then nodded fast.

"I knew it!" smirked Kyra, as me and Kellie started giggling. "*You're* in love with *Ja*-cob! *You're* in love with *Ja*-cob! *I'm* going to phone Billy and *tell* him! *I'm* going to phone Billy and *tell*—"

Bedoiiiiinnnnngggggg...

Kyra's sing-song teasing stopped dead at the sudden loud noise outside the window. *Right* outside our *second-floor* window...

"It was probably an owl," said Alan, five minutes later, after he'd stuck his head outside the window and then closed it and fastened it shut again.

"But it went *bedoiiiiinnnnngggggg*," I told him, realizing as soon as the words were out of my mouth how dumb that must have sounded. I was about to try and explain myself by adding "I didn't know owls went *bedoiiiiinnnnngggggg*," but I think I'd have ended up sounding like even more of a doughball.

Still, he seemed to understand that's what I meant.

"Yes, but there's a fire escape right outside that window," he explained, ruffling a hand through his ruffly-looking hair. All the teachers had looked a bit ruffly when the four of us had gone tearing along to the staff room just now, begging for help. (I think the ruffly thing had something to do with the empty bottle of wine I spotted on the coffee table...)

"So?" shrugged Kyra, in her usual, unsubtle way.

"So, I think an owl might have landed on the fire escape, and that's what the noise was!"

"Oh!" said Kellie and Sandie in unison, from the safety of Kellie's bed, where they were both hunkered together under one duvet.

Somehow, I didn't feel so convinced. Were owls really all that keen on perching on metal fire escapes, when there was a whole world of tree branches out there? I'd have to consult a top animal expert on that (i.e. ask Tor when I phoned home tomorrow night).

"So ... if you girls are all right, I'll leave you to get to bed," said Alan, padding for the door in his trainers.

"Thanks! Goodnight!" Kyra called after him in that sweet/sarky way she uses for winding teachers up, as Alan pulled the door closed on us. "Hee hee! What a laugh!"

"Kyra, I don't remember you laughing too much when we heard that noise!" I snapped at her out of nerviness.

"I didn't mean *that*! I mean, what a laugh that we're all going on about fancying Alan, and next thing he's in here! If he only knew!"

OK, I got her point then, and cringed and sniggered along with her and Kellie and Sandie.

"Still, glad it was just an owl..." Kyra admitted, once the cringes had died away.

"Yeah, it's not like it was anything weird or anything," Kellie chipped in.

"It was silly of us to get jumpy, wasn't it?" said Sandie, though I noticed she hadn't exactly legged it back to her own bed yet.

"Fancy leaving the light on all night?" I suggested.

You've never heard three girls say "Yes!!!" so enthusiastically...

Chapter 10

PASS THE TOTAL SHAME, PLEASE

"Ally, could you pass me the cornflakes?"

The girl speaking – that was Marie Whitfield from the other geography class at my school. Poor Marie was one of the suckers who'd ended up being shoved in the same group as Feargal and Mikey D for this week. I was so sorry for her I almost felt like handing her a sympathy card as well as the cornflakes.

"There you go," I said, shoving the box down the length of the long dining-room table.

"Um, Ally, don't know if you've noticed," Kyra drawled from the other side of the table from me, "but you've just passed Marie a jug of orange juice..."

Oops.

You know, I think I was still more asleep than I was awake. The way I felt, I guessed I must have had about ... ooh, *thirteen* minutes sleep last night. Maybe fifteen, if I was lucky. That was partly because it was pretty hard to nod off with a big, bright overhead light blasting through my eyelids, but I suppose it was also partly because I was still a bit spooked about what *might* have been out there on the fire escape, if it wasn't an owl, like Alan had tried to assure us it was. (A burglar? A blood-sucking vampire bat? A badger with no fear of heights?) Also, the fact that Kellie had night-mares – well, more night-*mutterings* – for hours and hours didn't help. Every time I felt like I might *just* manage to snooze off, she'd start tossing and turning in her bed (hard to do – there wasn't much room since Sandie was still in it), mumbling stuff like, "No! Get those feathers out of my face!" and "Shoo! *Bad* owl! *Bad* owl!".

My head felt so gloopy with lack of sleep I didn't know how I was going to manage to concentrate on our project work. Thank goodness for Warren Murphy, whose one brain was smarter than all of the rest of ours put together...

Speaking of Warren, through the fog in my befuddled head I suddenly heard his name being mentioned.

"Hey, Warren! What d'you think the chances are of you making someone's Top Three Boys list?"

Noooooo...! I panicked, flicking my gaze over Kyra and Sandie's shoulders to the table right behind them, where a grinning Feargal O'Leary was lightly baiting a squirming Warren Murphy. At the same time, he was staring directly at *our* table.

" 'Cause I don't think *you'd* get on any girls' Top Three list."

"Omigod!" mumbled Kellie beside me, her heart obviously sinking as much as mine was as a horrible, *confusing* realization dawned on us.

"Well, not any of the Top Three lists *I* heard," Feargal continued, while Mikey D snickered by his side.

"How did he...?" squeaked Sandie in a whisper beside me.

Exactly. How did Feargal know anything about our Top Three Boys lists? He couldn't have heard anything! Unless ... omigod ... *unless* he'd crept up the fire escape last night, and listened in on us, till a squeaky metal step went *bedoooiiinnnggg* and gave him away...!

"It's like, *you're* on that list, right, Jacob? And so are *you*, Nick. And so's –"

Kyra sure can move fast. Before Feargal got a chance to come out with the third name (oh, the shame if he had!), she'd screeched back her chair and towered in front of him threateningly, like a skinny bolt of lightning.

"You are in *so* much trouble, Feargal O'Leary!" she snarled. "I'm going to tell the teachers that you were spying on us last night!"

"Ah, come on, Kyra – don't tell! I was just having

a laugh!" pleaded Feargal, following her out of the room so fast that his hood fell down.

We could still hear him trying to joke her out of ratting on him as she stomped down the corridor in her cork wedge sandals.

But it was too late. It didn't matter whether Kyra told on him to the teachers or not; everyone in the entire dining room – including the two old ladies who were filling the tea urns and wiping the tables – knew our business. Most people might only know that our combined Top Threes included Jacob and Nick, but from the awkward, embarrassed look on the boys' faces at Feargal's table, Jacob, Nick, Marc, Warren and Mikey D had all been told last night that we'd also talked about fancying Alan.

And if that wasn't horrifyingly, mortifyingly, gut-churningly awful enough, we were also being laughed at (and no, not just by Mikey D).

"I'd like to pour that box of cornflakes right over their heads!" Kellie whispered angrily, as she scowled in the direction of a sniggering Lisa, Danni and Martha.

I'd have preferred to chuck the orange juice over them instead. But I didn't know if I'd have time to do that before the earth opened up and swallowed me in total *shame*...

Chapter 11

THIRD BUSH TO THE LEFT...

Marc and Warren were really nice guys. I mean, *really* nice guys.

We'd been stomping about some rocky bit of hill with them all morning and they hadn't said a *peep* about the Feargal fiasco at breakfast. Not one tiny dig about the Top Three Boys lists. But then again, maybe that's because they were terrified of Kyra after seeing her raging at Feargal. Now *that* would make sense...

"Where's this stupid limestone quarry meant to be?" growled Kyra, using her clipboard to swat a bunch of midges away from her face.

Like most things with Kyra, the midges were her own fault. She'd squooshed herself in so much body spray this morning before we left the dorm that she must have smelled like a mobile perfume factory to her tiny insect fan club.

"Well, according to the map, if we just follow this path through the wood, it'll bring us right there," said Marc, pointing a sausage-sized finger at some dotted line on the floppy map in his hand, while trying – I noticed – to slow down his huge, lanky stride so the rest of us with mere *mortal* legs could keep up. Warren, tap-tap-tapping his pen on his scribbled notes, nodded in agreement about the direction we were going in. Or maybe he was just keeping time with the tap-tap-tapping.

"It's a bit spooky here, isn't it? With all these trees, I mean," Sandie murmured, glancing all around her.

"Well, you do *tend* to get a lot of trees in woods!"

That was me, trying to be funny, but realizing it had come out sounding a bit sarcastic. Guess I was still kind of tired – *and* stressed from this morning's humiliation in front of everyone. Feargal's exploits on the fire escape had caused real ructions – not only did he get hauled in to the staff room for a stern rant, but before we set off on our day's project work everyone on the trip had to listen to a lecture that went along the lines of *never* go out on to the fire escape 'cause of safety issues (unless, of course, there happens to be a large inferno in your room). Nobody had said anything but everyone *knew* that the lecture was all because of Feargal creeping up the fire escape and listening in to us discussing our lists. Honestly, standing there in the hall right then I'd felt as vulnerable as if I'd only been wearing my knickers and dog-chewed bra in public.

"Ally…?"

Uh-oh, sounded like one of Sandie's famous favour requests was on its way.

"What?"

In reply, Sandie slowed down a little, deliberately dropping behind the others and waving me to join her.

"Ally – I don't know what to do…"

For a second, I worried that she was about to start whingeing about the rotten mobile reception again, but then I could tell by her pinched face that something was definitely *wrong*.

"What's up?" I whispered, noticing that Kyra was glancing back over her shoulder to see what was going on.

"It's just … it's just that I … I need a wee. I mean, really, *really* badly!"

"Well, go behind a tree, then!" Kyra bellowed, before I could get a subtle word in. (Actually, I'd have said exactly the same thing, only a few decibels quieter.)

"Oh, but I *couldn't*!" said Sandie in pink-cheeked alarm.

"Course you can! Everyone does it in the country!" I tried to reassure her.

"But maybe I could wait till we get to the old quarry?"

"Thing is, Sandie," I grimaced, "it's an old quarry. It's just full of rocks and stuff. There's not going to be any loos there – only lots more people since that's where we're meeting everyone. So it's going to be even *less* private trying to go for a wee there!"

"Oh..." mumbled Sandie, looking like she might cry, or faint, or wet herself. "I guess I'd better be going now then..."

"Yeah, go and find a big bush. We'll all wait for you further up the path," I told her.

"Not *too* far, Ally!" Sandie called out in alarm, as she began stumbling through the undergrowth.

"Watch out for the bears!" Kyra called out wickedly, before I could catch up with her and slap my hand over her mouth.

"And no peeking!" Sandie's voice trailed off as she rustled invisibly somewhere in the greenery.

"We won't!" Kellie yelled back.

"Yeah," said Kyra. "Better make sure you're far enough away so Marc and Warren don't get a flash of your bum! *Ow* – what was that for, Ally? I was just having a laugh!"

You know, she deserved every midge bite, bramble scratch and arm-thumping going...

But apart from our humiliation earlier and Kyra's tendency to moan and tease, I'd been enjoying this morning. The way Alan and the other teachers had set it up, all the groups were given a different route and map to set off and do our projects, so we'd been all by ourselves, with no sniggering and knowing sideways glances to put up with. Unlike Sandie, I wasn't particularly in any hurry to leave this pretty, "spooky" wood behind and face everyone down at the quarry.

Still, the idea of yet more humiliation didn't seem to bother Kellie too much, not now her tummy had started rumbling.

"It's not too much further, is it, Marc? I'm starving!" said Kellie, already drooling at the thought of the picnic lunch the teachers had promised would be waiting for us all at the quarry.

"Don't think so," Marc shook his head, turning the map this way and that, just to make sure. Don't know why he was bothering doing that though; he might as well have stood on his tiptoes – then he'd have been practically tall enough to see past the trees and check out where we were.

"It better not be too far – my feet are *killing* me!"

Er ... no wonder Kyra's feet were killing her. She'd just walked three and a half kilometres over open countryside in her cork wedge sandals. She couldn't understand when Alan had groaned at the sight of her minuscule denim shorts and chunky sandals this morning, just as we were about to set off. "But I'm wearing socks this time!" she pointed out, as though pink-and-silver-lurex striped ankle socks were the footwear of choice for mountaineers everywhere. They went really nicely with the fierce red bramble scratches on her bare legs though.

"By the way," Warren suddenly began, totally out of the blue, after hours of saying not much unless it had something to do with our geography project. "We tried to tell Feargal not to do it. To sneak up to your room last night, I mean. But he didn't listen, and Mikey D kept egging him on."

"Well, thanks for trying," I shrugged, pleased that Warren and Marc had tried to stick up for us, but kind of wishing he'd stuck to saying nothing about it, so I didn't re-live the shame all over again.

"What about the other two?" asked Kyra, bending to try and slacken the strap of her sandal that was currently slicing through one of yesterday's blisters. "Jacob and Nick? Did they think it was a big laugh?"

"Nah," Marc shook his head. "They thought it was a duff idea too."

"And what did they say when Feargal told them we'd..."

Kellie's question trailed off as she realized how embarrassing the end of it was going to sound.

"They didn't laugh when he told them," Warren jumped in, understanding exactly what Kellie was asking. "I mean, they looked a bit chuffed, but they didn't make a big joke out of it or anything."

Well, that was a small consolation, I guess. We had to see those two for the whole of the rest of the week, and I didn't fancy staring at my shoes solidly for the next three days just to avoid their eyes. (Though I'd probably still do that anyway...)

"God, I'm going to need more plasters," grumbled Kyra, pulling down a sock to inspect the damage.

"Maybe there'll be a First Aid kit in one of the minibuses the teachers are picking us up in," I suggested, trying not to gag at the sight of Kyra's weepy raw flesh.

"There *better* be. Oi! *SANDIEEEEEEEE!* Hurry up! Pee faster! I need to go and get patched up!"

In response to Kyra's roar, there was ... nothing.

"Sandie? SANDIE!?" I called out louder.

Nothing.

"Sandie? Where are yooooou?" Kellie took a turn.

Nothing.

"*SANDIEEEEEEEEEE!*" Marc bellowed, doing a great impression of a human foghorn.

Nothing.

"Sandie! Can you hear us?! *Sandie?*" I called again in a panic, hurrying down the path a little nearer the spot where I'd seen her go step-stepping over the tumble of plants and bushy bits.

"Omigod," sighed Kyra. "The silly moo was so shy about having a wee that she's wandered into the woods and got lost!"

"What are we going to do?" I asked, feeling my blood run cold.

"What's her mobile number?" asked Warren, pulling his own phone out of his pocket.

Kellie fired off a whole bunch of digits at high speed.

"But it probably won't work – she's been having trouble getting a signal," I babbled, watching Warren intently as he waited for a ring tone.

"Nah – you're right," he said, shaking his head and pressing his phone to "off". "Don't know how I'd have managed to give her directions anyway, if she's lost."

True. He could hardly have told her to "take the first left at the third tree from the right" when presumably Sandie was now surrounded by about a *hundred* of the things.

"What are we going to do?" I said again, since it was the only thing to say.

"We've got to go and get Alan and the other teachers!" Warren announced, taking charge of the situation. (Thank goodness one of us had a fully functioning brain.)

"But ... but shouldn't we try and search for her?" Kellie suggested.

"No – we could *all* get lost," said Warren. "We should just leave a marker here – like a cross made of stones or something – just to show where we last saw her, and then come back with the teachers."

"Yeah, we're only a few minutes from the quarry!"

I saw Kyra take one decisive step forward, then buckle over in pain.

"I can't walk! It's too sore!" she whinnied, reaching for her tortured heel.

"D'you want a piggyback?" Marc offered. (A knight in very tall shining armour...)

Kyra looked him up and down warily. She might have joked about the idea of Alan giving her a piggyback yesterday, but she didn't seem so sure about Marc.

"Dunno ... I might get vertigo," she mumbled.

"Well, maybe you should stay here – in case Sandie manages to find her way out on to the path."

"Are you joking, Warren? This place is *way* too spooky!" Kyra shuddered, before grabbing Marc by the shoulders and bounding on to his back quicker than a jockey on a horse at the Grand National.

"...and then we were shouting for her..."

"...but she didn't answer..."

"...'cause she must have gone really far into the woods..."

"...yeah, she didn't want anyone to see her weeing... *Ow!* What did you do that for again, Ally!"

"OK, OK, OK!" Alan put his hands up to slow the three of us down. "Let's start again. What exactly's going on?"

No wonder Alan seemed confused. There he was, standing in the quarry, sipping a cup of tea out of a plastic cup, quietly admiring the scenery before all the groups turned up for lunch, when me, Kyra and Marc had come hurtling out of the woods at him like a runaway psycho circus troupe (Marc carrying Kyra on his back probably looked like a tumbling act gone wrong, while I – madly flapping the map – must have resembled a manic clown doing an origami trick badly.)

"Sandie's lost in the woods!"

I couldn't pant it plainer than that. Even though saying it made me feel like runny raspberry jelly inside.

Alan frowned, then glanced round and waved

Miss Moore to come over. "And where's the rest of your group?"

"Warren and Kellie decided to stay on the path, just where we last saw Sandie!" Kyra explained, staring down intently at the top of Alan's head from her lofty position.

"What's going on?" asked Miss Moore, hurrying over from the minibus and staring round at us all (she was probably wondering if the circus really *had* come to town).

"One of the kids has gone missing," said Alan in a voice that was so horribly serious, I felt sick. "We'll have to get everyone together and get a search party org—"

I saw it. I saw straight away what had made Alan grind to a sudden halt. A figure – no, *two* figures – coming down another path that led out of the woods.

"Sandie!" I yelped happily, hurrying over towards her, as she limped slightly down the rubbly path, leaning hard on none other than Jacob.

"Found her in the woods a few minutes ago!" Jacob called out to whoever might be interested, which of course was *all* of us. "It's all right! She's OK!"

Thankfully she did look pretty OK. Maybe just a bit lightly grazed around the edges. I could just make out a faint scratch on her cheek and some twigs in her hair. Oh, and a happy-to-be-found smile too.

And that sweet little smile was in sharp contrast to the faces that I clocked next, appearing right behind Sandie and her rescuer. It didn't look to me like Lisa and her Clique were *remotely* happy to have helped find my friend in the big, bad woods.

"Are you all right, there?" Alan asked, beating me and Kyra to it and striding over towards Sandie.

"Uh-huh. I just got a bit lost. The trees all looked the same!" Sandie explained, as Jacob gently helped her step over a chunky tree root, handling her as if she was as delicate as a dandelion clock.

"We heard her shouting for help," Jacob carried on with the explanations. "I recognized her voice, and I kept shouting back till she found her way towards us."

Sandie gave her hero a shy smile, and didn't seem in any hurry to stand on her own two feet, even if all she appeared to be suffering from was that scratch and some serious hair-rumpling. Walking directly behind Sandie and Jacob, the Clique had managed to swap their sour expressions for blank ones – for Alan's sake, presumably, since they wouldn't want to sully their goodie-goodie reputation in front of a teacher.

"But how did you get separated from your

group?" Alan asked Sandie, giving her a once-over glance for any major damage. "You know the rules – everyone's meant to stick together!"

"I ... uh ... don't really ... um..." Sandie mumbled awkwardly, her face flushing instantly, understandably pink. I mean, I know everyone in the world has to wee, but I guess Sandie didn't really want to blab what had happened and leave Alan and Jacob with the mental image of her flashing her little white bottom in the undergrowth.

"She was trying to pick some wild flowers!" I blurted out, aware that Kyra and Marc were shooting me "Huh?" glances.

Good grief ... how unconvincing was that? Making Sandie sound like she'd just strolled out of a Jane Austen novel! ("Oh, Papa! I've plucked these wondrous forget-me-nots just for thou!")

Still, it (amazingly) did the trick.

"Hmm, OK," grunted Alan, gazing from me to Sandie. "Anyway, you look all right, Sandie, but I'll get Miss Moore to run you back to Tarbuck House to get checked over, just to be on the safe side."

As Alan turned to talk to Miss Moore, a dart of bitchiness snapped through the air.

"Picking flowers?" hissed Lisa, just loud enough for us, but not the teachers, to hear. "Bet she was having a *pee*!"

"Yeah – better check that she hasn't got loo roll hanging out of her jeans!" snorted Danni.

Kyra had been bending over to rub at her blistered heel, but as soon as Danni came out with that disgusting comment, she snapped up straight, opening her mouth to lash back with something I suspected would be even *more* disgusting. But before Kyra got a chance to jump to Sandie's defence, Jacob played the part of her rescuer again.

"Yeah? And what were you doing behind that tree earlier, Danni – looking for fairies?"

Now it was Danni's turn to pinkify in the cheek department. Sandie might have appreciated Jacob standing up for her, but right now I think the frosty-faced Clique might have been wishing she'd *stayed* lost in the woods...

Chapter 12

NABBED AND NOBBLED

Something was bugging me.

"Cilla's got a knot in her fur."

"Has she? Can you brush it out?"

"Nope. Too hard."

"So..." My mind ticked fast, trying to ask Tor a relevant question. It wasn't his fault that everything that had happened here today had been so mad that a story about a bunny having a bad hair day back at home in Crouch End wasn't exactly holding my attention. But it wasn't this that was bugging me. "So, you'll have to cut the knot out, right?"

"Uh-huh. Rowan wants to do it but I won't let her."

Fair enough. If Rowan got her hands on Tor's rabbit, she'd get carried away as usual and next thing, Cilla would be modelling some cutting-edge mini-Mohican or something.

"Are you going to ask Michael to cut it?" I quizzed him, thinking of our lovely, friendly neighbour, who was Superman disguised as a vet to my kid brother.

"Mmm. D'you want to talk to Ivy?"

"Go on, then!"

As I waited on the phone for Tor to go and track down Ivy I glanced at my watch: it was nearly 7.30 p.m. – i.e. nearly time for as all to gather in the TV room, where Alan was laying on a "special treat". I hoped Ivy wasn't in the middle of a bedtime story by now. I didn't want to disturb her in the middle of *Snarlyhissopus* or something equally important.

And so I waited. And waited. And waited some more, and all the time, all I could hear down the phone was the distant babble of our TV, plus a bit of a snuffly breathing sound, which was probably down to one of the dogs giving the receiver a passing sniff. But all the time I waited and listened to the background burblings from home, something was still bugging me. It wasn't the Clique's bitchy remarks when Jacob came out of the woods with Sandie – I mean, that *was* bugging, but it wasn't what was bugging me now. And it didn't have anything to do with the fact that me, Kellie, Marc and Warren had had to carry on with the project this afternoon without Kyra and Sandie, 'cause they got taken back to the sick bay to be checked over. That was all right really, once I knew Sandie was OK, and anyway, Kyra was being more of a limping hindrance than a help to the work we had to do. (By the way, after she'd been checked over, Sandie spent a happy afternoon texting Billy from the comfort of an armchair, while me and the others were comparing *lichen*, for goodness' sake...)

Nope, it was something else entirely that was bugging me, if only I could figure out what it was. And then I sussed it.

Badda-badda-badda-badda, badda-badda-badda, badda-badda-badda, badda-badda-badda-badda...

What was that annoying noise? It was like someone slapping you on the back of the head non-stop. Stepping back so that the swirly-whirly phone cable stretched right out, I could see where the noise was coming from. It was a baseball being battered on the ground, by Feargal O'Leary, who was apparently leaping around and using the gunshot-bouncing of the baseball as a way to stop Warren from getting through the doorway of the TV room. Every time Warren leant one way to try and slip past, a grinning Feargal would frantically *badda-badda-badda* the baseball right in his path.

"Feargal! You want to shut up that noise! Can't you see Ally's on the phone?!" Kyra bailed me out, swanning barefoot from the games room across the huge hallway towards the TV room, and spotting the whole situation at once.

With a quick glance in my direction, Feargal sullenly did what he was told, and even stood aside to let Kyra by, followed quickly by Warren who'd spotted his chance to escape.

"Come on, Ivy..." I mumbled softly, turning my attention back to my phone call. What was taking so long? The "special treat" Alan had promised would be starting any second now.

"S'me! Ivy!"

At the sound of my little sister's voice I jumped. And then it dawned on me; that funny snuffly sound that I thought belonged to the dogs? It was the sound of Ivy breathing. When Tor said he'd go and get her, she was probably standing right beside him. She must have been silently hovering at the other end of the phone for the past couple of minutes, just waiting for me to talk. What an adorable, weird little kid...

So I *had* to talk to her, of course. I told her all about what a good time Mr Penguin was having, and about the snail race some of the boys organized in our break this afternoon (no world sprinting records broken, as you might guess), and then I heard from her about the drawing she did that day (apparently, it was red ... and green ... and pink ...

and orange ... and a very long list of other colours).

In fact, I babbled on so long to Ivy – and then to Dad, who'd come to get Ivy to go to bed – that I totally missed the start of the "special treat" in the TV room. But even from the passageway I managed to make out what it was; a video of the movie *Volcano*. Alan must have picked that 'cause it tied in nice and neatly with the geography theme or something. Bet he trotted it out every week, for every new batch of kids coming to Tarbuck House. I didn't know about anyone else, but I'd seen that video ages ago, so it didn't really fit into the category of "special" or "treat". Actually, I reckon a lot of other people must have felt the same way, since I spotted plenty of restless bods out of the corner of my eye, all heading past me towards the loo and back again, just to break up the monotony. One restless bod in particular stuck her tongue out at me cheekily as she sauntered by – but then it *was* Kyra Davies so I just carried on chatting to Dad and stuck my tongue out right back at her.

After I finally hung up, I was just about to go over to the TV room, when I heard Kyra's voice drifting from further back along the corridor. Which is not hard to do since she speaks at full volume at all times.

I assumed she was in the girls' loos, but when I

reached there, I heard another cackle of laughter (Kyra, definitely) erupt from one of the classrooms just ahead of me – i.e. one of the classrooms that were supposed to be out of bounds when we weren't studying in them.

"Yeah, you're right! He definitely has a crush on her!" Kyra was saying, as she perched on the teacher's desk, her plastered bare feet swinging back and forth. It took a couple of steps into the darkened classroom for Kyra to spot me – and for me to spot who she was chatting and joking with...

"Hey, hi, Ally! God, isn't that film too old and boring to be true? I was just saying to Feargal that I never managed to watch it all the way through the first time I saw it!"

"Oh..."

Yes, "oh" was all I managed to say. What I really wanted to blurt out was, "Why are you hanging out with an annoying idiot like Feargal O'Leary, like he's your oldest friend?". But the annoying idiot was currently sitting on the desk opposite Kyra, staring at me hard, smoking a cigarette and trying his best to intimidate me (which was working, by the way).

"But then we got gossiping!" Kyra carried on regardless, as though Feargal hadn't crept up the fire escape last night and spied on us, or hadn't been winding up poor Warren only twenty minutes or so ago. That girl really must have the short-term memory of a bluebottle...

"What about?" I mumbled, wandering a wary couple of steps closer to them both.

"About Jacob! Fancying Sandie! He's definitely got a crush on her – Feargal heard him talking about her to Nick, didn't you, Fearg?"

"Fearg" said nothing, but just nodded, and blew a stream of smoke in the air. I coughed.

"Anyway, apparently Jacob was saying something about her being really pretty and everything. And you should have seen them in the TV room before the movie started, Ally! He was all, 'How are you now, Sandie?', and 'Are you OK?' He even made Kellie move over so he could sit next to her!"

"Did he?" I gasped, suddenly so caught up in this most excellent gossip that I forgot to be fazed by Kyra being so buddy-buddy with Feargal.

Snap!

The room was flooded with instant sharp light, and I whirled around to see Alan in the doorway, with one finger on the light switch and a look on his face that didn't exactly say "Hi, guys! Good to see you're having fun!".

Nobbled. That's what my dad said he called it at school, when teachers nabbed you for doing something wrong, and I was sure that was just what had happened to me now.

"Didn't I say – during the intro talk yesterday – that these rooms were out of bounds in the evenings?" he stated sternly. (It's actually quite hard to look teacherly-stern when you're wearing a Foo Fighters T-shirt, faded jeans and old Converse baseball boots, but Alan was doing a pretty good job despite that.)

"Uh ... yes," I mumbled bleakly, and heard a similar mumble coming from Kyra and Feargal too.

"So why do I get told you three are in here?"

I dropped my gaze to the floor and frantically wondered who'd bother to go ratting on us.

"And not only are you three in here, but you're in here *smoking*!"

Shocked, stunned, shamed ... that was me.

Shocked at being accused of smoking (never done it), too stunned to answer back and defend myself (Me? Argue with a teacher? I don't *think* so!) and full of total shame, shame, shame at getting into trouble. And so I just hung my head lower, and listened to the anti-smoking lecture that Alan was blasting out at us.

"OK," he said at last, "you can go. Get through to the TV room and see if you can stay out of trouble. Right?"

"Plonker..." I thought I heard Feargal say, as he barged through the classroom door and led the way down the corridor and across the big hall.

Luckily, Kyra kept her mouth shut, and only did a disgruntled roll of her eyes in my direction, just as we walked into the TV room, which was thankfully pretty dark – so no one turning around to watch us walk in could see how red my face was.

But what I instantly spotted was the twinkle of three gold "name" necklaces, as the Clique swivelled round in their chairs to gawp. And snigger. I heard them.

And then I knew instantly who'd ratted on us and got us into trouble with Alan...

Chapter 13

SANDIE GETS THE WRONG SORT OF FLOWERS

It turned out that Mr Penguin wasn't the only stowaway in my bag.

Later, when I was looking for some spare (sensible) socks to lend Kyra for the next day, I came across a marble, a piece of Tor's *Jungle Book* jigsaw, a purple felt-tip pen (with the top thankfully on), a packet of doggy crunchies and a scrunched-up note that said "lov Ivy" in wibbly-wobbly kiddie writing. I'd have to thank my little sis for her kindness when I phoned home tomorrow night.

"It's *my* fault that they're hassling you lot now too," said Sandie mournfully, as she walked across to her bed, neatly ducking the socks I was chucking at Kyra.

"Forget it!" Kyra told her matter-of-factly, as she stretched up and caught the chucked socks. "Like I said before, they're a bunch of morons. Who cares?"

Kyra might not care, but Sandie obviously did – she was really mortified at the Clique landing us in trouble with Alan tonight, whichever one of them it was.

And *I* cared too. It was horrible to think people disliked you so much that they got a kick out of making your life a misery, all because … because what? Because of something as dumb as Sandie bagsie-ing this room first? It didn't make sense…

"Those three are such *idiots*," Kellie grumbled from her bed, scooping up her tiny braids with their teeny-tiny beads into a messy, scrunchied top-knot. "I mean, what's with them dressing almost identical all the time? And those matching name necklaces – what's that all about?"

"They're probably too thick to remember each other's names any other way," Kyra muttered, as she examined my plain white socks like they were *toxic* or something.

"Anyway, forget them," I said, noticing that Sandie had only managed a feeble smile at Kyra's jibe. "What about lover-boy?"

At that, Sandie went crimson, and froze, just as she was about to pull the duvet back on her bed.

"Billy?" I carried on, wondering what Sandie's slapped-face expression was all about.

"Oh, *Billy*!" she suddenly smiled, visibly sinking with relief. "I thought you meant *Jacob*! 'Cause …

'cause Kyra called him lover-boy yesterday. Y'know, when she was teasing me!"

Excuse me, but Sandie was acting *weird*.

"Er ... I was just going to ask how many times you texted him today."

It was a simple, silly question. I'd only asked it because I thought talking about Billy would cheer her up after the Clique's efforts at being spectacularly unpleasant today.

"Um..." Sandie shook her head and frowned. "I dunno ... um ... must have been about ten times, I thi—"

Wow, Sandie's message count was *well* down today, even with her textathon session this afternoon. But that point was kind of overshadowed by the fact that she'd just pulled her duvet back, and found something pretty surprising underneath...

"OK, girls, sleep well," said Alan, bundling the muddy sheets and duvet up in his arms. "And no more dramas, please – you lot have given me enough grief!"

He was smiling as he pulled the door closed, but I was still cringing at his words. I hated the fact that we now had this reputation as severe pains in the bums as far as he (and the other teachers) were concerned. I mean, apart from losing Sandie today *and* getting a telling off for "smoking" in the classroom tonight, we'd already dragged him out of the staff room this time yesterday, 'cause of the Feargal-shaped "owl" out on the fire escape.

"*Us* giving him grief!" Kyra scowled, and kicked at the mattress that Alan had turned on its side to dry out. "What a *joke*! What about whoever dumped a flowerpot in Sandie's bed? *They're* the ones giving the grief round here!"

"And three guesses who sneaked in here and did it!" said Kellie, crossing her arms angrily as she sat on her bed.

"Yeah, but we can't *prove* it!" I pointed out, holding my duvet up so Sandie could double up with me for tonight, since her own bed was unusable. "And you heard what Alan said when you mentioned Lisa's name!"

He'd just laughed, and then shrugged off our "wild" allegations. You could tell he never thought Lisa and her mates would have done it in a million years – he said it was probably one of the boys larking about. Actually, I had a funny feeling that he thought it was Feargal again, but somehow – and it wasn't as if I wanted to take Feargal's side ever – I didn't think this *was* down to him. Chucking a soggy pile of earth and a half-dead chrysanthemum in Sandie's bed wasn't his in-yer-face, wind-up style. It was just plain *mean*.

"Ally...?" Sandie whispered, ten minutes later when we'd finally put out the lights.

"Uh-huh?" I mumbled a reply, feeling her shivering a little beside me.

"What did I do to deserve that?"

"I don't know, Sandie," I whispered sadly back, as I forfeited most of the duvet and tucked it around her to keep her warm...

Chapter 14

RAIN, RAIN, GO AWAY ... (I WISH)

"I'm going over there," said Sandie, pointing to a small hillock a few metres away, where Marc was currently standing shaking a compass, like it had run out of batteries or something.

"What for?" I asked, pulling one squelching boot out of a particularly muddy bit of riverbank.

Like I needed to ask...

"I'm going to see if I can get a signal for my phone up there, so I can text Billy!"

Ah, Billy. If Billy could see me now he'd laugh himself stupid. Even *more* than the time he dared me to do the splits in the park and my jeans ripped apart at the seam. (It wasn't splits gone wrong that he found so funny – he just loved the fact that I had to walk home sideways with my bum against garden walls so nobody got a flash of my whiter-than-grey knickers...)

"Good luck!" I mumbled after Sandie, as she headed off to join Marc. (Maybe she hoped he'd act like a giant radio transmitter?)

"What are these ... *things* called again?" Kyra snarled, holding out the tent of yellow plastic material she was swamped in.

"Kagoules," I muttered, looking at Kyra as the rain dripped off my eyelashes and realizing that however hideous I felt, she was suffering much, *much* more. Not only did she have to wear this standard-issue, Tarbuck House, wet-weather gear, but Alan had forced her to put on a size-too-big pair of proper, clumpy, fashion-free, hill-climbing boots he'd dug out of some cobwebby cupboard for her. "They'll be fine with a couple of pairs of these," he'd told her this morning, holding out some knarly, thick socks that looked like they'd been hand-knitted by sailors' wives at the turn of the century. The *fifteenth* century...

"You know, they're not really kagoules – they're actually rain capes," Warren butted in, gazing up from the notes he was making on his clipboard, under the shelter of the giant golf umbrella Kellie was holding over him.

"Warren – shut it," Kyra said spikily, while pointing a (wet) warning finger at him.

She wasn't in the mood for idle chit-chat. She was barely even in the mood to speak to me, Sandie and Kellie, she was so hacked off at the weather and the sailor socks.

None of us was too thrilled with the sheets of rain we'd woken up to this Wednesday morning, although maybe Feargal and Mikey D weren't too bothered since it was legitimate hood-wearing weather. We weren't exactly in the mood to tramp around a soggy moor and riverbank all day either. Double maths in a nice dry classroom would be like heaven by comparison… (Er, sort of.)

"'Ooh! They're actually *rain* capes!'" a voice suddenly mimicked Warren. "Ooh, give's a twirl in your lovely *rain* cape, Warren!"

Warren glowered at Feargal, and looked like he really wanted to say something, but was trying to stop himself. Poor guy – what must it be like for him to have to share a room with morons like Feargal and Mikey D? I didn't see them picking on Marc too much, but I guessed that might have something to do with him being the size of the Eiffel Tower. And I bet they didn't take the mickey out of Jacob and Nick either; I bet they tried to be all matey with them, since they were pretty cool.

"Yeah! Give's a twirl, Woz!" Mikey D joined in, slouching over from the rest of his group, who were busy scrambling around by the riverbank, taking measurements, just like all the other groups were doing. (Watching from a distance, it must have looked like a bunch of mutant bananas were on the loose around the river.)

"Yeah, c'mon, Woz!" said Feargal, trying to grab Warren into a waltz or something.

"Don't!" I tried to say on Warren's behalf, but Feargal didn't seem to hear me – there was too much rustling of plastic "rain capes" going on.

"Not going to give us a twirl? Look, I'll even give you a hand!" Feargal cackled, still trying to grab at Warren.

Now Feargal was taking it too far. He was such a pain. How could he be so mean to Warren? It suddenly occurred to me that maybe I shouldn't have given him the benefit of the doubt last night – maybe he *was* mean enough to sneak into our dorm and chuck that flowerpot into Sandie's bed. I turned round to see if Kyra was maybe thinking the same thing, but was a bit stumped to see that she was grinning. How could she go sniggering at Feargal winding Warren up so badly?

Er, she wasn't, as it happened...

"Check it out!" said Kyra, pointing at something just over my shoulder, I realized, milliseconds before I started scolding her for something she wasn't *actually* doing (oops).

"It" was Sandie, who had now been joined by a smiling Jacob, holding out his mobile phone to her, leaving Marc standing there like a very tall lemon. With a compass.

"And check *that* out!" Kyra continued, turning slightly and nodding her head at three girls in rain capes standing not far behind Mikey D. They were recognizable only from their sour, pale faces, which were now tuned like satellite dishes to the situation with Jacob and Sandie.

"Are they jealous?" I wondered aloud. "Does one of them fancy Jacob or something?"

"Bet you a zillion pounds that's *it*," Kyra announced. "OK, so Sandie nabbed the room from them, but it's *more* than that now!"

Getting side-tracked by the shenanigans with Sandie, Jacob and the Clique, me and Kyra had momentarily taken our eyes off what was happening right in front of us. And what seemed to be happening was that Feargal was still determined to manhandle Warren into spinning round, and managing at the same time to jostle Kellie and her umbrella out of the way.

"Oh!" she gasped, as she struggled to keep her balance in the slippy-slidey earth. I leant forward and caught her by the elbow to steady her, but even though she didn't end up on her bum in the mud, Warren went mental. (Well, as mental as someone gerbilly like Warren can get.)

"You stupid *pillock*!" he raged at a dumbstruck Feargal, then pushed him really hard.

Just like Kellie, it looked for one wobbly moment there that Feargal was headed for an unexpected mudpack on his nether regions, but unluckily he managed to stop himself – by crashing into Lisa, who went slithering backwards down the riverbank with a loud and very, *very* funny "*Eeeeeekkkkk...*" as she disappeared from sight.

Like everyone around, we all stood frozen for a second, locked in shock in case she was hurt *and* struggling not to laugh at the most comical disappearing act anybody had ever seen.

But before we could run to help, or burst out laughing (whichever came first), Lisa's head popped up, like a startled meerkat wearing a mud-pack, and that was it – we were *gone*; lost to a tidal wave of giggles that was as unstoppable as a double-decker bus hurtling down a hill with bust brakes.

Through the rain and my tears of laughter, I could see Danni and Martha scowling our way, but there was *nothing* (and I mean nothing) I could do about it...

Chapter 15

SAVED BY AN ARMPIT

I tell you, my grandma was *obsessed*.

"Sausages and mash."

"And?" she quizzed me.

"Er … that was it."

"What – no vegetables?"

"Well, some peas, but they were a bit hard."

"Hmmm…"

But even if my grandma *did* have an unhealthy obsession with my diet, I was actually quite glad to chat to her about snoozeville stuff like the daily menus at Tarbuck House, even if it did mean that everyone queueing behind me for the phone thought I was having the most dreary conversation in the entire history of the universe. The reason I was glad to chat to Grandma about nothing in particular (same with Mum earlier, when we joked about how long it was going to take Dad to fix my bedroom door) was because it meant that I didn't have to tell them what was *really* going on. The fact was, I couldn't bear for anyone in my family to know about all the trouble I was (accidentally) getting into.

Like what happened today with Alan hauling up our whole group – plus Feargal and Mikey D – after Lisa's tumble in the mud. Even though it was Feargal who had bashed (OK, stumbled) into Lisa, I think Alan decided that because me and my friends were always getting into hassle, we must have encouraged Feargal or something. Course, being caught laughing didn't help us look particularly innocent but it wasn't really fair for Alan to pick on us for that, seeing as everyone else in all the other groups was sniggering just as hard. Not that he liked that much either – we were *all* in his bad books.

"Anyway, I better go, Grandma. There're loads of people waiting to use this phone."

"All right, Ally, dear. Now remember, you don't have to call me tomorrow – I don't expect you to call every night!"

(Translation: "You don't have to call me tomorrow night, but I'd be really, really pleased if you did!")

"OK. Bye Grandma! Say bye to Stanley for me!"

Urgh … I felt another *ping!* of homesickness then – homesickness for Grandma's pretty, hyper-neat flat with its puffy cushions and framed photos of us stacked everywhere, and her cat Mushu to play with and Stanley to joke around with and Grandma herself handing round her biscuit tin that was always magically full (unlike ours at home). Instead, tonight, we were all going to be imprisoned in the TV room, forced to watch some dull-as-a-dentist-visit educational film, as punishment for our general bad behaviour on the field trip today.

As I stomped along the corridor in the direction of the TV room, I was staring blankly down at the tips of my trainers – lost in gloomy thoughts – and nearly jumped when a hand swung out in front of me, barring my way.

"Hey – better tell your friend to back off!"

I was being "spoken to" (a nice way of putting it) at close range by one of the Clique, but I was so thrown for a second that I couldn't remember which one it was, never mind figure out which friend I was supposed to tell to back off. (And back off *what* exactly?)

Flicking my eyes down to her neckline, I saw from the name necklace that she was Danni. And very quickly, Danni spelt out exactly what she was hissing on about.

"Your stupid mousey mate better lay off Jacob *right* now!"

Speed-of-light thoughts skidded around in my

mind as I tried to come up with a response to that poisonous little outburst. For a start, how dare she call Sandie "mousey"; second, what business was it of hers if Sandie was friendly with Jacob? But then I remembered some advice Grandma once gave me after I'd had a run-in with Claire Franklin in primary school (horrible little minx who was trying to tease me about Mum vanishing). "When idiots like that try and bait you into an argument, Ally, don't even *try* to fight back – you don't want to stoop to their level. Just walk away and leave them rambling to themselves."

So that's what I tried to do now. Maybe I wanted to jump to Sandie's defence, and maybe I was curious about what Jacob had to do with anything, but it wasn't worth wasting a second talking to delightful Danni about it.

"'Cause Jacob is Lisa's, OK?"

It turned out I wasn't being *allowed* to walk away – Danni's arm was still barring my way, blocking my escape route along the corridor. And despite Grandma's excellent advice, I found my mouth saying stuff before my brain had even finished *thinking* it.

"Jacob's going out with Lisa?" I frowned, a bit gobsmacked by that news, since I'd never seen them doing what normal people do when they're dating, i.e. hanging out together. Or even talking, when it wasn't anything to do with the geography project their group was working on.

"Well, *no*," shrugged Danni, still not dropping her arm. "But Lisa saw him first, and she's fancied him for ages. So tell your friend to get her hands off!"

Huh? Sandie had never had her hands *on*!

"For *your* information," I heard myself saying in a slightly shaky voice, "Sandie isn't interested in Jacob *that* way. She's got a boyfriend!"

(Sorry, Grandma – I couldn't keep my mouth shut...)

"Doesn't look like it to *me*!" Danni snapped in my face. "Not the way she's *always* talking to him and sucking up to him!"

Er, OK, so now I wished I'd done what Grandma said and walked away – or at least ducked under Danni's outstretched arm. I really didn't want to end up in some no-win slanging match. But how was I going to get out of it?

With the help of an armpit and Feargal O'Leary – that's how...

"Phew! Wanna get a bit of deodorant on that!" smirked Feargal, appearing from the close-by boys' loos and pretending to bend over and sniff under Danni's outstretched arm.

I don't suppose for a second that Danni (or the

other two in her Clique) smelt anything other than fragrant in the armpit department – they were too prissy and perfect not to deodorize, or whatever the proper word is. But Feargal's teasing did the trick – outraged at being accused of having BO, Danni dropped her arm to her side super-speedy, though with that glower she gave Feargal it seemed like she was toying with *raising* it super-speedy and giving him a swift bonk on the nose for his cheek.

But she wasn't about to do that with a certain teacher suddenly looming at the end of the corridor.

"Guys!" Alan called out brusquely, clapping his hands together. "TV room, quick as you can! Video's going on in one minute!"

He didn't need to tell me twice. I zoomed off, desperate to get away from drongo Danni and very, *very* desperate to go and sit with my sane friends and tell (well, whisper to) them about the madness that had just gone on.

"Feargal – hood down, please!" I heard Alan order, just behind me, followed by a loud tut and sigh.

You know something? I felt kind of guilty for not saying thanks to Feargal for rescuing me just now. But the problem was, I didn't want to come across all matey with Feargal – I was getting a bad enough reputation without getting lumped in with him. Then it struck me – duh! – Feargal hadn't wound up Danni to help me out; he'd done it just 'cause it was fun to wind her up! Hadn't he?

I dunno … Feargal and his natural talent for landing himself – and anyone nearby – in trouble; the Clique and their ridiculous idea that Sandie had a crush on Jacob. Urgh … and it was only Wednesday night, i.e. two more days of possible hassles and bitchiness and muddy stomps across moors ahead. I wished I could wiggle my nose and bewitch myself into Friday afternoon, when I'd be safely back at home, in a wonderful world of comfy chaos, bedrooms with no doors on and bra-chewing dogs…

Chapter 16

TROUBLE? STEP THIS WAY...

Things to do when you're trying to stay out of trouble:

1) Stay out of trouble.

2) Er, that's about it.

Things to do when you're trying to land yourself in even *more* trouble:

1) Let Kyra Davies talk you into something really dumb.

"Come on, we'll sit on the stairs and stare at the stars!"

Better still, we could just stare at the stars from our dorm window and forget about the stairs altogether.

"Kyra, I don't think we should be doing this..." I muttered, standing on the cool metal of the fire-escape platform and trying not to go wibbly at the sight of two floors' worth of thin air visible between all the criss-crossed metalwork.

"It's too hot in there! What's the harm in us sitting out here for five minutes to cool down?"

I didn't know what the harm was, but every harmless thing we'd done this week so far had turned into some major hassle, so I didn't see what would be different now.

"It's all right, Ally," said Kellie, as she slithered out of the window after me and Kyra. "The staff room's all the way downstairs, on the other side of the building, so as long as we speak quietly, no one'll hear us!"

Speak quietly? Wasn't Kellie forgetting something – i.e. Kyra "Foghorn" Davies?

And it didn't matter if Kyra was right about our room feeling like a sauna tonight. I mean, *yes*, after raining all day, the weather *had* turned hot, sticky and steamy, and we *had* felt like sticky toffee puddings flopped on our beds chatting, but sneaking outside was a seriously bad (if tempting) idea.

So if I thought it was such a lousy idea, how come I let myself be persuaded to do it? Standing there in my checked blue and white PJs on the gently creaking metal platform directly outside our dorm window I asked myself the same question. And the answer was a great big fat "Dunno..."

"Is this thing safe to take our weight?" said Sandie, warily taking her turn after Kellie and placing a white-socked foot on the platform.

"Well, it better!" said Kyra, already padding

down the stairs. "It's meant to take the weight of zillions of people stomping down it in the middle of a fire, so the four of us shouldn't be a problem!"

"And *us*!"

We froze.

That voice; it did *not* belong to an owl.

As Kyra, Sandie and Kellie gawped frantically at each other and all around, something made me gaze down. I dropped on to my haunches and saw six (six!) sheepishly grinning male faces gazing up at me from the platform below. The boys from the dorm downstairs had obviously done the same thing we had and sneaked out for some air. Though why the likes of Warren and Marc and Jacob and Nick had wanted to hang out with Feargal and Mikey D in such a small space, I had no idea. If I were them, and had to put up with Feargal and Mikey D's constant wind-ups all the time, I think I'd have been tempted to let those two scramble out of their room window first – and then lock the thing behind them...

"Hi, Ally!" Feargal waved up at me. "Hey, nice nightie, Kellie!"

Kellie – the only one of us girls not wearing PJs – frantically gathered up the material of her swishy, lilac cotton nightdress. It was so dark that the boys probably hadn't got too much of a eyeful of her matching lilac knickers, but she wasn't about to risk it.

"Wanna come down?"

The sensible thing to do of course was say "no" to Feargal's totally resistible offer. The *sensible* thing would have been to clamber back into our room, and carry on where we'd left off before Kyra had come up with her sudden, dumb idea about the fire escape – chatting about the hideousness of the Clique and teasing Sandie about her texting score for today (only seven, but it had been a busy day, what with getting into trouble and everything).

So, did we do the sensible thing? Ho, ho, ho...

One minute later, the four of us were parked on the last few steps that led on to the boys' first-floor metal platform. Us girls were all scrunched up, with our knees self-consciously held to our chests, while the boys just looked like a tangle of gangly legs, all bent or stretching out for what little space there was. Although it seemed rude to look too closely, they all seemed to be dressed in T-shirts and boxer, or football shorts (and hooded tops, if you were Feargal or Mikey D, worn unzipped for a bit of ventilation on this hot night). The one thing I could have *sworn* was that Warren's top looked *exactly* like something the crew in *Star Trek* wear, but I wasn't about to say that out loud, just in case

Feargal hadn't sussed that yet and would add being a Trekkie to the list of stuff he took the mick out of poor "Woz" about.

"We were just saying, pretty good laugh, wasn't it?" said Nick. "When Lisa did her mutant mud monster impression!"

"Serves her right – she's such a witch," grumbled Kyra. "Hey, you know what she got her mate Danni to say to Ally tonight?"

I felt a little shudder on my back, where Sandie's leg was pressing. I knew what she meant: Kyra did *not* want to blab that information in front of Jacob, not if she didn't want Sandie to shrivel up on the spot and die of embarrassment. The trouble with Kyra is that she's one of those speak first/apologize later kind of people. I had to act fast.

"Don't waste time speaking about any of that lot, Kyra!" I burst in cheerily. "They're not worth it!"

Kyra stopped and frowned at me, trying to figure out why I was trying to quit a conversation that we'd been engrossed in for the last hour or so up in our dorm. She wasn't the only one staring at me intently – so was Feargal. Oo-er … had he actually *heard* what Danni had been saying to me? Was he listening before he came out of the loo? Nah, no chance. If he'd heard, he'd have started in with the digs by now, or at least blabbed all about it to Jacob. And from the friendly but blank-ish expression on Jacob's face, he didn't have a clue he'd been discussed during the evening, let alone "claimed" by Lisa.

"Dare!" Feargal suddenly announced, switching his dark-eyed gaze from me to Kyra. "Dare you to a race across the lawn and back!"

"How?" Marc butted in, gazing from their platform to the ground below, which wasn't linked by a useful set of clunky metal stairs, but by a whole lot of empty space.

"They'll have to use *that*," said Warren, pointing to a folded metal ladder fixed to the side of the platform. "You release that and it extends, like a fold-up umbrella."

"See? Easy!" grinned Feargal, already bounding to his feet. "You up for it, Kyra?"

"Course!" she snorted, pushing up the sleeves of her red pyjama top like she meant business.

"Kyra!" I hissed, knowing that trying to get her to stop now would be as dumb as waving a slice of cold turkey in front of Rolf and Winslet and expecting not to have your hand practically bitten off as they lunged for it.

"It's OK, Ally!" said Kyra, standing by impatiently as Nick and Marc began to release the creaking, screeching ladder down. "I'll win no problem. Specially if I get a head start!!"

"Hey! No *way*!" Feargal called out, as Kyra cheekily bolted on to the ladder before it had even been half-way lowered.

And then, *whoooooossssshhhhhhh!*

Just as Feargal threw a fist down and tried to make a grab for Kyra and stop her from cheating, it was as if a very small storm cloud had settled directly over the fire escape and chucked down a week's worth of rain on us in one fell swoop.

Above our gasps (and a couple of swear words from the boys) there was the definite sound of ... giggling. And I may not be too hot at geography, but even *I* know that cumulonimbus clouds do *not* giggle.

As we dripped and shivered, we all stared up and saw three near-identical grinning faces peeking out of a third-floor window.

"Uh-oh, check it out – a torch!" mumbled Marc, alerted to a blast of light on the lawn from the corner of his eyes.

"It'll be a teacher – quick, run!"

You'd think the people from PlayStation had suddenly announced they were handing out free games consoles to the first bunch of teenagers to bag them. You have never seen anyone move so fast – except for Kyra, who was dangling from the half-lowered ladder, her hands scrabbling to pull herself up.

"Ally! Help!!"

Call me a mug, but when I saw the desperation in her face, I couldn't just scarper up the stairs and leave her there. Unfortunately.

"Here – grab my hand!" I hissed, and I leant down towards her in the dark. "No, don't do that! *Aaaarghhh!*"

And then the whole night seemed to light up, as we were caught in the glare of Alan's powerful torch; Kyra's skinny legs still pedalling madly in thin air, me with my pyjama top half over my head 'cause of Kyra yanking at it as she tried to pull herself up.

"Going somewhere, ladies?" Alan's stern voice called out.

Yes, I thought, with my head wedged inside some blue and white checked material. *Planet Shame*...

Chapter 17

ER, WHERE EXACTLY ARE WE?

Now I knew how a mouse felt.

Alan was watching us like a *hawk*. When we got on one of the minibuses that took us to the coast this morning, when we stomped about the beach – same as everyone else – making notes about the jagged cliffs towering over us, whenever we scratched our noses, he'd be clocking us, ready to pounce on us if we did *one* thing wrong.

Me and Kyra, we'd got off with a warning last night. Our official crime? Breaking safety regulations, "*and* spoiling his boozy night with the other teachers, I bet!" Kyra mumbled later, when we'd padded up to the dorm via the proper indoor staircase. "Did you smell the beer on his breath when he was talking?" To be honest, I was so ashamed at getting a warning that Alan could have been dressed as the back end of a pantomime cow and I'd have still been freaked out. "And what about the water? He didn't care about that, did he?"

No, Alan hadn't been particularly interested in the fact that "someone" had chucked a bucket of water on us for a laugh, or the fact that anyone else had been out there on the fire escape with us. "Kyra, I only saw two people on those stairs – you and Ally – so there's no point trying to shift the blame; it won't help your case."

At the beginning of this lunchbreak, though, we got a bit of time off from being watched by our very own grunge-style prison guard; one of the girls from Westbank went into the sea for a paddle which turned into a soaking when a wave decided to play a practical joke on her and shove her over. Alan was now on his way back to Tarbuck House in one of the minibuses, with one very soggy and miserable girl wrapped up in a travel blanket beside him. Amazingly, he hadn't assumed me or my friends had anything to do with this disaster (a miracle, since he blamed us for everything else).

"Notice something weird?" said Kyra, watching as Jacob taught Sandie how to skim stones across the top of waves.

"What's that then?" I asked, scrunching up the packet of crisps I'd just finished.

"The whole time we've been stopped for lunch, Sandie hasn't taken her mobile out of her bag *once*."

"Yeah – and she didn't take it out any time this

morning when we were walking along the bottom of the cliffs!" Kellie butted in.

"Hey, Ally," Kyra turned and looked questioningly at me. "She *is* still going out with Billy, isn't she?"

"Course!" I burst out defensively, even though a little voice in my head had been whispering, "What's she up to?" all the time Sandie had been talking (and laughing, and stone-skimming) with Jacob.

"Y'know, I don't mean this in a horrible way, but boys didn't really look at Sandie before, did they?" said Kellie, letting a handful of pebbles rattle through her fingers.

"How d'you mean?" I frowned. What was this; Have-A-Go-At-Sandie Day?

"Well, I just mean, lads didn't seem to fancy her till she started going out with Billy, did they?"

"S'pose," I shrugged. Sandie had always been kind of pretty, but pretty like a little girl's doll – all big eyes and shy-sweet. Like Kellie had said when we were round at Kyra's house on Saturday, Sandie had definitely got a bit more self-confidence since she'd been dating Billy. Maybe – to boys – that tiny bit of extra confidence made her seem less like a doll and more like a real girl...

"If Jacob doesn't have a full-on crush on her, I'm a hippopotamus," Kyra mumbled, her eyes again glued to the giggling and stone-skimming going on by the water's edge.

"Hey, where's the Clique?" I asked, suddenly realizing that there didn't seem to be any laser-beams of hate firing in Sandie's direction right now.

"Are you speaking about Lisa and that lot?" asked Marc, scrunching up beside us and towering so high he blocked out the sun.

"Yes, we *are* talking about that bunch of witches," said Kyra, tilting her head back as she gazed up at Marc. "Why?"

"Coven," interrupted Warren, appearing out of Marc's shadow.

"What?" Kyra glowered at him.

"It's a coven. Of witches, I mean. That's the proper word – not 'bunch'."

Kyra shot Warren a wilting look and then turned her attention back to Marc. "So, go on – what were you going to say about them?"

"We just saw 'em; they're in the shop at the beach car park. There's a couple of tables in there, and the teachers are sitting at one of them –"

"– and Lisa and the others are sitting at the other one," Warren added.

"Sucking up," growled Kyra. "It figures..."

"Anyway," Warren began again, "The teachers

were saying lunch is over. We've got to get back to work. Look, they've given every group a different bit of the project to do this afternoon."

"Whoop-dee-do..." said Kyra drily, without even looking at the piece of photocopied paper that Warren was holding out for us to see.

"Right," I said, pushing myself up off the stony beach, "I'd better go and drag Sandie away from Billy..."

"Billy?!" laughed Kellie. "You mean *Jacob*!"

Yikes! How could I have got the two of them muddled up like that? Weird ... I was still obviously in a state of shock after what had happened to me last night and my brain was malfunctioning (a little bit more than usual).

"Tell 'em what he did to you this morning."

That was Marc, nudging Warren jokily, but because Marc is so big and Warren is so gerbilly weedy, Warren had to reach out and steady himself so he didn't fall off the end of the picnic table and benches our group was all crammed around.

"What? What did he do to you?" Kyra asked, already grinning at whatever rotten trick Feargal had pulled on poor Warren *this* time.

"He pulled the laces out of my trainers when I was sleeping, then pretended he hadn't done it."

Feargal O'Leary – what a master comedian. I *don't* think.

"So did he give them back in the end?" I asked, trying to brush away the hair that was slapping across my face. (It was really windy up here at the car park at the top of the cliff.)

"Not *exactly*," shrugged Warren. "I had to go down to breakfast with my trainers flapping."

"Couldn't you have worn another pair of shoes?" asked Kellie.

Her hair was tinkling – actually *tinkling* – in the wind, 'cause of all those beads at the end of her braids.

"Nah – my boots got soaked in the mud yesterday."

"Forget that! Tell 'em what happened with your laces!" Marc nudged Warren again.

"Then at breakfast," Warren sighed, "Feargal acts all matey, and asks if my cornflakes are all right."

Me, Sandie and Kellie exchanged some confused glances. Kyra was less subtle.

"What did he ask that for?" she said bluntly.

"Well, I didn't know – till I looked down at the bowl of cornflakes and saw my trainer laces floating in the milk!"

"So that's why all those lads were laughing round

your table this morning!" Sandie announced. "I wondered what that was all about!"

God, boys can be so horrible, can't they? Not just Feargal, I mean (that goes without saying), but all the lads that were sniggering at Warren's predicament.

"Anyway, I put my laces back in and got my trainers tied," Warren continued glowering down at one foot. "Only trouble is, I tied them in a double knot when they were wet, and they've dried so tight I think I'll have to cut them off later..."

Uh-oh ... now *I* was being officially horrible, as Kyra started *one* giggle that started up a giggle lurking somewhere in *my* chest too. A couple of seconds later, and we were all giggling, even Warren, even though he was the butt of the joke.

"Hey – look at the time! It's nearly quarter to four! Where *is* everyone?" Kellie suddenly announced, once the giggles had finally rippled away.

Now we definitely didn't feel in the mood to giggle. Glancing around, it dawned on me – and everyone else – that we were the only ones in this car park, apart from two seagulls who were prancing along the path that meandered down the cliff like they were some middle-aged couple out for a bracing Sunday stroll.

Thanks to Warren and his brain, we'd finished our assignment early, and been the first to arrive at the car park, ten minutes before we were meant to meet up with the rest of the groups and the minibuses to take us back to Tarbuck House. But we'd been so busy yakking about last night, about the Clique chucking water and getting away with it, and Warren's trainer traumas this morning, that we hadn't spotted time creeping on – with not a minibus or another school group in sight...

"Where *are* they all?" Sandie blinked, looking slightly alarmed.

"Warren," said Kyra, narrowing her eyes at him. "It was *this* car park that we were getting picked up from, right?"

"Yes, definitely!" he nodded earnestly. "That's what she said! They'd changed the pick-up from the car park at the beach, to the car park up on the cliff!"

"Miss Moore definitely said *this* cliff, though, yeah?" I asked, casting around madly like some other cliff would suddenly lurch into view.

"Miss Moore?" Warren mumbled, looking confused.

"Yes, Miss *Moore*," Kyra said slowly and distinctly, as if she was spelling it out for someone particularly thick (which Warren certainly wasn't, as his near perfect exam marks always showed). "She's the teacher that told you, isn't she?"

She had to be. She was the only female teacher on the trip. Warren had told us "she'd" let him know about the change of pick-up point, when we'd set off to do our assignment after lunch.

"But Miss Moore didn't tell me!" he blurted out. "I mean, not exactly!"

"Well, who *did* tell you, exactly?" I asked quickly, aware that Kyra was on the point of pouncing over the table and shaking the information out of him.

"Uh ... M-M-Martha told me," Warren stumbled over his words, like it was dawning on him that something was wrong here. "She came up to me in the shop and said the teachers had changed their mind about where the minibuses would be, and they'd asked her to pass the message on..."

Warren Murphy. He might have the kind of brain that stores gallons of facts and figures, but that obviously didn't leave any room for common sense.

"Have we been set up?" asked Marc, who was beginning to catch on in the ways of the evil Clique.

"Duh!" Kyra exploded, rolling her eyes skyward.

"What are we going to do?" squeaked Sandie.

"Well, first," Kyra announced, stamping one borrowed, oversized mountain boot on the bench and starting to scramble across the table, "I'm going to *kill* Warren..."

Chapter 18

DANCING (AND PRANCING)

"Hurry up!" Kellie whispered to me, as she passed by me in the corridor on her way up to our dorm. "Got to get ready!"

That was a joke. How could I get ready for the last-night party when I hadn't known there was going to *be* a last-night party? They could have warned us so we could have packed something party-ish to wear. And yes, in my case something party-ish would probably be my best black cords instead of my mud-splattered jeans, but you know what I mean.

"Yeah, in a second..." I mouthed at her, pointing to the phone I was holding to my ear, as I listened to a familiar voice prattling away, long distance.

"Let's see ... what's been happening here..." mused Rowan. "Well, I finished my new coat today, but I'm a bit fed up."

"Why, don't you like it?" I asked, starting to twirl the phone wire around my fingers (and getting in a bit of a knot, if you must know).

Maybe Rowan had tried her coat on and spotted her resemblance to a yeti.

"No, I *love* it! It's just that the weather's too sunny and nice to wear it, that's all."

So, she liked being a purple yeti, then.

"How's Linn?"

"Grouchy. But only low-level grouchy, so that's OK."

"What's she grouchy about?"

"She caught Ivy squirting her new hair-straightening serum over Rolf. But you know what she's like – she can't stay mad at Ivy or Tor for very long."

True. If it had been me or Rowan she'd caught wasting her precious hair serum like that, she'd have torn our heads off. Near enough.

"And what did Rolf end up looking like?" I asked, imagining our scruffy, hairy dog panting patiently while Ivy dolloped gloop all over him.

"Smooth. Anyway, Mum finished a new sculpture today."

"Did she?" I loved hearing about Mum doing her artwork. Somehow it meant she was properly home, properly settled. "What's it of?"

"Er ... she said something about it being a baby marmoset, hanging on to its mother's back."

Phew, I was glad Rowan had told me that. I

could picture Mum's sculpture now; it would be one brown blob with a smaller brown lump on top of it. But if I knew what it was supposed to be, I could act more convincingly impressed when she showed it to me once I got back home.

"So ... what've you been up to today, Ally?"

Urgh ... I was dreading this question. What could I say? How about, someone played a particularly mean practical joke on me and my mates and left us stranded in a car park in the middle of nowhere. And 'cause no one could get a signal on their mobiles, we'd all had to trudge down to the nearest (and only) building in sight, which happened to be a country pub, and beg for help. Mr Martinez coming and picking us up in a minibus half an hour later ... that was fun (not). We got a lecture about letting Palace Gates School down, which came just *before* the lecture Alan ended up giving us about responsibility when we finally got back to Tarbuck House. And then there was the fact that the teachers didn't believe for a second that golden-girl Martha had spun a line to Warren; he must have "picked her up wrong".

No, I wasn't in the mood to tell Rowan all that, mainly 'cause I just wanted to forget it, and count down the hours till tomorrow morning when we could escape this place and head back to Crouch End and my pleasantly mad family...

"Oh, hey! I nearly forgot!" Rowan suddenly burst out, before I was forced to tell her anything about my horrible day. "Billy called earlier – he wants you to phone him. He says it's urgent!"

Urgent? What could be urgent with Billy? Had he got himself a new skateboard? Was he dying to tell me he'd beaten Hassan at Giant Jenga? Had Precious got his poodly head wedged through the trellis in Billy's back garden again? That's the sort of rubbish my friend Billy considered "urgent" news. (The doughball.) But hey, I guess I'd kind of missed speaking to him all week, even if the last time I'd seen him he'd done my head in wittering on and on about Sandie.

"OK, I better get off and call him," I told Rowan, relieved to change the subject.

I wasn't so relieved ten seconds later, when I realized what Billy was going to change the subject *to*.

"...and she only texted me seven times yesterday, and I texted her *twelve* times!"

"Yeah, well, we've been pretty madly busy, Billy," I mumbled, trying to excuse Sandie, and then sussing out that the last time I'd seen her, she'd been playing ping-pong in the games room with Jacob. "And the phone signal round here *is* pretty dodgy."

"Well, she managed to text me from someone else's phone on Tuesday. Whose was that?"

"Er … dunno. Some girl from the other school that's here." I lied a bit, hating myself for doing it.

"You know how many times she texted me today, Al?"

"No."

"Zero times, Ally. She didn't text me *once*."

"It – it must have been the signal," I heard myself faffing. "It must have been really bad today. I'll go upstairs right now and check with her."

"Ally, you would tell me if there's something going on, wouldn't you?"

Urgh … fibbing to Billy was as horrible as teasing Colin our cat for only having three legs. And I wasn't even sure if I was fibbing or not, since I wasn't exactly sure what was or wasn't going on with Sandie and Jacob. I wasn't even sure if *Sandie* knew what was going on with her and Jacob.

"It's cool. I'll get her to call you, no worries," I replied, vowing to frogmarch Sandie to this payphone just as soon as I got Billy off the line. Even if she didn't have any money, I'd *lend* her some. "But listen, I've got to get off now 'cause there's a big queue of people waiting to use the phone."

The corner of my mouth always twitches when I'm lying, and it went into twitch overdrive as I said bye and put the phone down on Billy, and walked away along the empty corridor...

It didn't matter how much Alan jigged about behind his toytown-looking DJ console. It didn't matter if he'd set the lights either side of it to flash yellow, green and red in time to the music blasting out. No one was dancing. No one was moving a muscle, apart from to chat, cross-armed, to the friends they were huddling together with.

"Is this a *joke*?" winced Kyra, sticking her fingers in her ears. "Is this the Tweenies or something?"

"No – it's the Cheeky Girls," Warren informed her, straightfaced. "It's called 'Touch My Bum'. It was a big hit. Don't you remember it?"

"I think she's been trying to forget it," I told him gently, as Kyra rolled her eyes at Warren's total sense-of-humour bypass.

And you know something? You really needed a sense of humour with the music "DJ" Alan was playing at our party tonight. Who'd have guessed that a youngish Liam Gallagher lookalike, who wore T-shirts with cool rock bands' names on the front, had such hideous taste in music? Practically everything he'd played so far was *pants*. (Including the Cheeky Girls, who were just two stick insects in *silver* pants, if I remembered their video right.) Or maybe the problem was that he thought 13 year olds like us had hideous taste in music. (Uh, I don't *think* so!)

"Hey, Ally," Kellie nudged me at that moment. "What do those three *look* like?"

It was pretty funny. Like me, just about everyone had been taken by surprise at the idea of us having a last-night party, and were basically wearing the least muddy T-shirts, jeans and trainers that we had. The exception to this was Kyra (but her flared mini, wedge sandals and pink and silver ankle socks were just day-to-day, bog-standard clothes for her), and the Clique. They were now standing over by the window, with ironed hair, tiny vest tops, smart black trousers and strappy high sandals, way too much make-up and matching aloof expressions.

"Pillocks!" I muttered to Kellie, with a grin on my face. "They must think they're in the audience for *Top of the Pops* not in a grotty games room surrounded by foldaway ping-pong tables!"

"Jacob looks nice, though!" Sandie suddenly butted in, gazing over (adoringly?) in the direction of Jacob and Nick, who were rifling through Alan's CD collection in what was probably a vain search for something decent to request.

"Have you phoned Billy yet?" I cut in, bursting Sandie's bubble with a timely reminder.

"No! I forgot!" gasped Sandie, slapping a hand to her mouth.

"Again?"

I knew my voice had an edge to it, but it had been over an hour since I told Sandie I'd spoken to Billy, and that he wanted her to call him. She'd been blow-drying her hair in our dorm when I first mentioned it. She'd looked horrified at the idea that she'd completely forgotten to contact her boyfriend all day (and quite right too – even if their normal lovey-doveyness made me feel a bit squeamish sometimes). I hadn't liked it when Kyra and Kellie started teasing her, saying she'd forgotten Billy because she was too busy with Jacob. To be exact, it wasn't their teasing that bothered me – it was the fact that Sandie had gone pink and giggly when they'd started up…

"I'll go and phone him *right* now," Sandie assured me, fixing her big blue eyes right on me.

Oops … now I felt rotten for hassling her. Sandie couldn't help it if she was kind of dippy, *or* if Jacob had a crush on her – she was probably a bit flattered, and why not? But when it came down to it, she was crazy about Billy (who knows why!) and felt horribly guilty now for neglecting him. Hopefully.

"This," Kyra suddenly announced, taking her fingers out of her ears as Sandie scuttled off, "is officially the most rubbish party I have ever been to."

After that proclamation from Kyra's sparkly-glossed lips, me, Kellie, Marc and Warren stared hard at her, wondering what was coming next.

"So we're going to liven things up, all right?"

Maybe we all looked too confused for her. Or plain scared. Whatever, next thing, Kyra was rolling her eyes again (she does that a lot) and stomping her wedges in the direction of Feargal O'Leary…

"What's she saying to him?" Kellie whispered.

"Don't know," I whispered back, as I watched Kyra talking directly into Feargal's hood.

But one thing was for sure … that was a big, wide grin he gave her there, as well as a thumbs-up.

Hmmmm…

"What are they doing?" squeaked Kellie in shock, as Kyra and Feargal threw their arms together, their noses in the air, and began doing something that was supposed to be a waltz-style thing, I guessed.

Everyone was staring at them, mouths hanging open in shock.

"Come on, you guys!" Kyra grinned wickedly over Feargal's shoulder as they swooped past us to the strains of "Touch my bum! This is life!".

"You have *got* to be kidding!" murmured Kellie, before finding herself practically swooped off her feet by Marc.

She flung me a panic-stricken look as he steered her towards the floor, and then she started cracking up laughing, as he spun her round so fast her Nikes weren't touching the floor.

"Well?" grinned Warren, showing me – for about the first time in my whole history of knowing him (not very well) that he *did* have a sense of humour.

"Well?" I grinned back at him, knowing we were milliseconds away from throwing ourselves around the room, necks held high and waltzing, like a cross between the meerkats at London Zoo and the original historical owners of this old, cobwebby house.

And that was it – we were off. It didn't matter that Warren's head only came up to my nose and that we didn't have a clue what we were doing. All that mattered was that we were holding on to each other for dear life, spinning around the room as fast as we could, and best of all, everyone was joining in!

OK, so not everyone fancied the grabbing-a-partner, waltzing option, but they were all making a stunning effort to dance as stupidly as possible, as *fast* as possible. As me and Warren spun past, I swear Marie Whitfield and some other girls from our class were pogoing like they were dancing to some punk record and not the Cheeky Girls, and – honestly! – I definitely saw Mikey D help some girl from Westbank School do a ballet-style pirouette. Apart from that, there was 50s twisting going on (Dad would have liked that, being a rockabilly at heart!) and daft 80s-style ravey little-fish, big-fish, cardboard-box moves happening.

Even when the music changed – when the Cheeky Girls segued into some cheesy, long-forgotten boy band "hit", the daft dancing didn't stop.

"All right, Ally?" Feargal laughed, as he grabbed on to my waist once Kyra had started off a conga line.

"Yeah!" I grinned at him. "But I'll be back in a minute!"

No, I *didn't* want to stop dancing, but I really *did* need to nip to the loo, so I grabbed Feargal's hands from round my waist and planted them firmly on the person who'd been directly in front of me (i.e. Warren – ha!).

And then I dizzily hurried off out of the games

room, aiming across the huge hall towards the girls' loos, hoping I could do what had to be done and get back again while everyone was still buzzing and silly. This doozy of a night (of a week!) was turning out to be such a laugh, thanks to Kyra and—

"Erk!"

At least, I *think* that's what I said, when I turned into the corridor and saw Sandie and Jacob.

Sandie and Jacob *snogging*, I mean…

Chapter 19

SQUIDGY SURPRISES

"You said you were going to phone Billy," I said flatly, lying (also flatly) on my bed and staring directly at the ceiling, i.e. not at Sandie in the next bed along.

"I know! I meant to! But then just when I started to dial, Jacob came along the corridor and he gave me this look that kind of paralysed me—"

"Like something the Borg would do in *Star Trek*?" I suggested, though I knew it sounded very, very sarky indeed.

"Maybe," I heard Sandie carry on warily, knowing I was very, *very* hacked off with her.

"So what happened then?" I heard Kellie ask, all dreamily, as if she was hearing the outline of the next Hollywood blockbuster, and not something that was going to crush my friend Billy's heart into tiny, bite-sized pieces.

"And then he just came towards me, and put his arms around me, and kissed me before I could even get the money in the slot!"

"*Awwwwwwwww!*" sighed Kellie from her bed somewhere on the opposite side of the room.

"Cool!" said Kyra, from her bed next to Kellie's.

But I didn't see anything "*awwww*" or "cool" about it. Didn't anyone here – apart from me – remember that poor, lovely, loveable buffoon in a baseball cap back home?

"Omigod – what's that?"

OK, so I was sulking (on behalf of Billy, of course), but even *I* couldn't resist sitting upright in bed to see what Kellie had just seen.

"Look!" squealed Kyra, legging it off her bed in the direction of the door, and the note that had just been thrust under it. Grabbing the folded piece of paper, she yanked our dorm door open and checked out the corridor outside it. "No one there!" she announced.

"Is it a love letter?" gasped Kellie, clapping her hands together.

"Let's see..." said Kyra, closing the bedroom door and flipping the folded paper around in her fingers. "Here, on the front ... it says ... 'Sandie'."

Both Kyra and Kellie let out an immediate squeal of joy and bounded towards Sandie's bed for a group hug.

But I couldn't join in; not when I knew that back

home was my amazingly stupid, brilliant, goofball of a best boy mate, who'd be angsting out big-time right now about what was going on, and why his girlfriend hadn't phoned him, especially when I'd promised to get her to…

"*'Sandie – please meet me downstairs in the TV room in five minutes'*," Kyra read out, a huge, infectious grin on her face.

"From who?" asked Sandie, like she didn't know.

"From … Dracula!" Kyra grinned inanely.

Sandie looked crestfallen.

"No – from *Jacob*, you idiot!" laughed Kyra, bouncing up and down on her knees on Sandie's mattress.

"Ally?" I heard Sandie call out, as Kyra and Kellie *both* began jumping gleefully up and down on her bed.

"What?" I asked dully, leaning on my elbows and gazing over at her.

"I really, really like Jacob!" she blinked her blue eyes at me. "I can't help it!"

Love … I'd read plenty about people who couldn't help loving who they loved, and it all sounded truly romantic – till it came to my best friend (Sandie) falling in love with someone who wasn't my other best friend (i.e. Billy).

But I didn't have much of a chance to mull that

over, since a ghost/giant owl/Feargal O'Leary started hammering at our window.

"What d'you want, Fearg?" asked Kyra, who'd inevitably jumped off Sandie's bed first, and thrown the window on to the fire escape wide open.

"You've been set up. Again!" mumbled Feargal, unself-consciously clambering through our window wearing only the latest Arsenal strip, without even a hooded top to keep him feeling cool.

"What are you on about?" asked Kellie, reining her legs in so there was room on Sandie's bed for Feargal to sit down.

"And why did you say 'again'?" I jumped in.

"Woz and Marc told me about what happened this afternoon," he told me, looking totally comfortable as he settled his long dark brown limbs across the top of Sandie's duvet. "And I know Lisa and that lot have it in for you guys."

How did he know? *Had* he heard Danni telling me to warn Sandie off Jacob in the corridor last night? And he hadn't used that info to *tease* anyone? Amazing...

"Hold on," frowned Kyra. "So you're saying we've been set up – you mean by Lisa and her mates?"

"Yep," he nodded. "I sneaked out on the landing

just now for a fag 'cause Woz was moaning about me smoking in the room –"

A fag. Urgh, I *knew* Feargal had to be up to *something*.

"– when I heard all this whispering going on above me on the stairs. So I nipped back into our room, but I kept the door open a bit so I could listen, and then I heard Lisa daring Danni or the other one to put something under your door..."

God ... so the note had nothing to do with Jacob?

"Then I saw her and Danni and the other one scurrying past, going on about 'getting Sandie' down in the TV room. So after that, I got straight on the fire escape up here, to let you guys know."

"We've got to tell!" Kyra announced, bounding off the bed. "I've got to tell Alan and the other teachers that Lisa and that lot are setting up an ambush!"

"Hold it!" said Feargal, reaching out and grabbing her wrist, bringing her to a standstill.

"What – you've got a *better* idea?!" I found myself snapping at Feargal, while still holding my duvet protectively close to my chest.

"Maybe!" Feargal eyeballed me with his intense dark eyes. "You want to go bleating to Alan and the other teachers and then they say you're mucking about?"

Er ... good point.

"Listen, I've got a plan. Just you all go and listen at the top of the stairs at the end of the corridor out there – OK?"

Blindly, I heard us all say OK, and then before we knew it, Feargal had hoisted himself out of the bedroom window and trampled back down the fire escape.

"Let's go!" grinned Kyra all of a sudden, waving us to follow her as she yanked open the dorm door and tiptoed her bare feet along the corridor, with all of us in tow.

"Stop!" hissed Kellie, hearing – same as the rest of us – an echoing, loud rat-tat of a knock somewhere down below.

"Yes?" said the distant, puzzled, sleep-heavy voice of one of our teachers.

"Please, sir!" said a voice in reply, which I couldn't quite place at first. "I've just heard some funny noises from the TV room! Maybe it's burglars?"

"That's *Warren*!" Kellie hissed, wide-eyed with sudden wakefulness and surprise, just like the rest of us.

"Well, I'd better check it out..." mumbled the other voice, which we realized had to be Alan's, as he plodded down the stairs.

A couple of barely breathing seconds later, we heard a terrible screech of voices, yelling, "*Got you, Sandeeeeee!*", followed by some wallops and splashy sounds – and Alan groaning.

"Water balloons, bet you five quid!" Kyra nodded, recognizing the telltale wet squidgy thuds we'd just heard, as the H_2O-filled plastic bags had slapped into Alan.

Q: How were the Clique going to wangle out of this one?

A: They weren't. Ha!

Chapter 20

TOP THREE BOYS LISTS, PART TWO

We'd finally escaped. I'd never been so glad to see a motorway in my life. In a few hours, I'd be back at home getting happily covered in pet hairs and dog drool. (Those dopey mutts of ours like to give everyone a welcoming lick if they haven't seen them for a while, i.e. anything over five minutes.)

Y'know, I didn't even care if I still didn't have a door to my room.

"Oi! Woz! What you sitting way down there for?"

"Feargal!" I winced, fearing for my eardrums as he stood by my seat and bellowed down the coach.

"Come on up the back! You too, Marc – me and Mikey saved seats for you!"

"Feargal O'Leary! Be quiet and sit *down*!" Mr Martinez turned and roared from his front seat next to the coach driver.

With a sulky tut, Feargal grudgingly did what he was told and stomped back up the aisle, slapping the top of each seat as he went. He was quickly followed by Warren and Marc, who dived out of their own seats, and with a nod and a grin to us as they passed, scurried up the aisle after him.

"Funny those two ending up all matey with Feargal and Mikey D, isn't it?" I turned and said to Kyra and Kellie, who were leaning over the top of me and Sandie's seats.

"I think Warren's just chuffed at having buddied up with a real-life bad boy!" Kyra smirked, as she dented the top of my seat with her elbows and rested her chin in her hands. "I think he even likes the fact that he's got this 'cool', nickname now!"

I guess through all the teasing and wind-ups, Feargal and Mickey D had got to know "Woz" and Marc bit by bit, since they were forced into sharing a dorm all week. But the turning point had come last night, with Warren helping out with Feargal's plan to land the Clique in it. (And *boy* did those three land in it – I think everyone in every dorm got woken up when Alan and the other teachers read the riot act to them. I think they were even too mortified to make it to breakfast this morning. The last we saw of "lovely" Lisa and her pals was when Miss Moore hurried them on to their coach to go home. They never took their eyes off the tips of their perfect trainers the whole time...)

"It's not just Feargal and Warren getting matey

that's funny," said Kellie. "*Loads* of funny stuff's happened this week..."

Sandie had been staring mournfully out of the window up to this point, but as soon as Kellie spoke, she swivelled her head around and gazed piteously at us all.

"I *know* you're talking about me. But please don't – I feel really bad!"

It was pretty obvious that Sandie felt bad – she hadn't said a word since we got on the coach fifteen minutes ago. All she'd done was rest her forehead on the cool glass and twist a piece of paper back and forth between her fingers.

"But why *exactly* do you feel bad?" I pushed her. I wasn't being mean by doing that – I just wanted to be sure I understood where her head was at. (I had a feeling it was as twisty as the bit of paper in her hand.)

"I feel bad because..." she faffed around, those spots of pink in her cheeks popping up, "...because ... I'm so *happy*!"

"Huh?" said Kyra, wrinkling up her nose in confusion.

"It's just that I feel so happy 'cause I met Jacob," Sandie started to explain, more animatedly. "And I'm so happy that he feels the same way about me –"

We could all see *that*. Even the *teachers* looked embarrassed at the farewell snogathon that was going on this morning before Jacob got on his coach.

"– but I feel *bad* because I shouldn't be happy about that. I mean, I'm going out with Billy!"

Er, ten points for remembering that fact, I felt like saying out loud, but I didn't – 'cause I'd lain awake for big chunks of last night, flipping the whole thing about Sandie and Billy and Jacob around in my head till I made some kind of sense of it.

"Thing is, Sandie," I began, "I know you've really liked going out with Billy –"

From the tense expression on her face, I realized that Sandie thought I might be about to have a go at her.

"– but you couldn't have liked him as much as you *thought* you did. Not really. 'Cause if you had, you wouldn't have fallen for Jacob, would you?"

Sandie blinked hard at me, and twisted the note in her hands till it looked like a paper plait.

"D'you think?" she asked me, in a soft, shy voice.

"Well, it's got to be, hasn't it?" Kyra blurted in. "I mean, you could've just fancied Jacob and stuck to that, and it would have been OK. But you went and actually snogged—"

"Yeah, yeah!" I shushed Kyra, thinking that she wasn't exactly helping me do what I was doing –

which was giving Sandie a way out of this mess, without her feeling too awful. And the way I saw it, it would be awful if she went back to Billy and carried on as if nothing had happened.

"You should finish with Billy, shouldn't you? It's not fair on him if you like someone better than him."

I felt a hundred per cent horrible saying it, but this was important – not just for Billy, but for mine and Sandie's friendship. If Sandie ended up still going out with Billy, when *I* knew the truth, I could end up ... well, *hating* her for making a fool of him. It was better to break up and hurt him rather than do *that*...

"OK," she mumbled, looking teary-eyed. "You're right, Ally."

I shrugged, feeling pretty wobbly myself. Poor Billy...

"But, hey – what are you doing!" I tried to say brightly, grabbing the mangled paper from her fingers. "You don't want to go tearing up Jacob's phone number, do you?"

Sandie gazed at me, stunned, wondering how I could have known that's what it was. But it hardly took a genius (which I certainly wasn't) to work it out, specially since I'd watched him write it down and give it to her, right before Nick dragged him on to the Westbank School coach.

"It's Jacob's number? Let me see!" grinned Kyra, scooping the paper out of my hand and unravelling it. "Why didn't he get you to key it straight into your mobile? Oh, *I* get it. He wouldn't have been able to doodle kisses that way!"

"Aw, cute!" Kellie giggled, sneaking a look at the piece of paper. "Hey – you should text him right now, Sand!"

"Later!" I said, grabbing the note back and slipping it into the pocket of Sandie's bag for her. (I might have helped her sort out her tangled love life, but I wasn't quite ready to sit next to her while she tapped a mobile love letter to her new boyfriend.)

"So, no guesses that Jacob's still number one on your Top Three list, then, Sandie?" Kellie grinned down at her.

"Guess he'd be at number two and number three as well, eh, Sand?" Kyra teased.

It was nice to see Sandie smiling again, even if it was a watery sort of smile.

"Tell you something!" Kellie suddenly dropped her voice and bent forward conspiratorially. "My Top Three's changed since we first did it!"

"Yeah, how?" I asked, dying to hear more, same as Kyra and Sandie, who were all ears and eyes and unbridled curiosity.

"Well, Alan's off it for a start!"

"Too right!" growled Kyra, as me and Sandie nodded in agreement. Given that he hadn't believed a word we'd said *and* had worse taste in music than your average two year old – well, both those facts sent him free-falling off *all* our lists.

"So who would be on your list now?" Sandie asked.

"Don't laugh!" grinned Kellie. "But I really like Marc!"

I could tell that Kyra was just about to squawk "Marc?" at a very high rate of decibels, so before she could embarrass Kellie in front of the entire coach, I reached up and slapped my hand over her mouth, while miming "Shush!" at her.

"I know it's mad – I never looked at him before!" Kellie carried on whispering, her brown eyes twinkling. "But he's kind of cute, don't you think?"

"Yeah, cute for a *giant*!" said Kyra, yanking my hand from her face.

"Talking about your Top Three Boys lists again, are you?" said a cheeky voice, as Feargal suddenly leered over Kyra's shoulder.

He never changed, did he?

"Sneaking around listening to people's conversations again, are you?" Kyra answered him back, narrowing her eyes and grinning at him.

"Might be," said Feargal, placing a hand on the

back of my seat and the other one across the aisle, then lifting himself up a little and swinging his feet back and forth in mid-air. "So come on, Kyra, who's in your top three?"

The cheek of him! Kyra narrowed her eyes even more and seemed to be considering a suitably sarky reply.

Then again...

"*You* are," she suddenly said, straight out, to Feargal's face.

It's fair to say that this particular statement came as a major shock to me, Sandie and Kellie, since Kyra had never given any hints about *fancying* Feargal. Yeah, she'd sort of said he was entertaining, but *fancying* him? Wow...

But if we were stunned, it was nothing compared to the effect it had on Feargal. For a second, he hung, suspended in mid-air, and then he sort of dropped his arms in shock and plonked his feet back on the floor, only not quite where he wanted them to be. There was a thunk, then a trip, and then an "*Ooooffff!*" as Feargal tumbled face forward on to the patterned aisle carpet.

Poor Feargal. I had my suspicions that he might be petrified at the idea of Kyra fancying him, and who could blame him...?

Chapter 21

CAKE, MORE CAKE AND SYMPATHY

"Welcome! Welcome! Welcome! Welcome! Welcome! Wel—"

"OK, Ivy, we've heard enough of that song now!" said Linn, handing our little sister a tiny piece of cake to distact her from singing her own special "welcome home" song for me, which consisted of one word – and one note.

"More cake, Ally!"

"OK, Ivy, sweetheart, I think Ally's had enough for now!" Mum smiled, swooping over and grabbing the squished bit of chocolate sponge from Ivy's fingers before she tried ramming it in my mouth.

Ahhh...

I was very glad to see everyone, and everyone was very glad to see me.

Ivy was sitting in my lap (the bit of lap that didn't have Rolf's head lolling on it), Tor had demanded to hear about the snail race I'd told Ivy about over the phone (I missed out the bit where

Marc accidentally stood on two of the competitors), Rowan had done a twirl for me in her new coat (yep, she did look like a big purple yeti), and Linn had baked me a cake specially (it was supposed to have had "Welcome Home, Ally!" written on it in M&Ms, but Winslet stole the packet and hid it somewhere).

And the gladness to have me home didn't stop there; Dad was closing the shop early specially and would be home soon, and Grandma and Stanley were coming round later for a celebration tea. You'd think I'd been gone on a year-long sponsored charity walk of the world, instead of spending five days trudging round fields, playing ping-pong and getting into shedloads of trouble. (Not that I'd told anyone about *that* yet.)

"So did you make any new friends?" asked Mum, scooping up Colin from the chair. (He'd nabbed that nice warm spot when she'd come to my rescue from the cake attack.)

I smiled, thinking how strangely everything had turned out. That very first day, I'd wondered if Lisa and her Clique would be our friends, but in the end it wasn't them I'd become friendly with at all (far, *far* from it). Instead I'd got to like Warren and Marc, who I'd known all the way through school so far but never got talking to *once* till this trip. And OK, so I'd got to like Feargal more too – but obviously not as much as *Kyra* had...

"Kind of," I answered Mum's question vaguely, mainly 'cause I'd just realized that – full of hassles as it was – the last week had been quite interesting and entertaining, I guess. In fact, five days ago I'd worried about having a lousy time at Tarbuck House, but in the end, it had turned out to be a pretty cool school trip after all.

Briiiiinnnggggggg!!!!

"Woooof, wooof, wooof, woooooof!"

"Wonder who that is?" said Mum above the din of Ben going crazy. (Doorbells, phones ringing ... they both send him barking mental.)

"I'll go," Linn announced, getting up off the other armchair.

But I'd quickly glanced at my watch, done a bit of mental arithmetic and guessed that it might be for me.

"No, don't!" I told Linn. "*I'll* get it – I think I know who it is!"

She'd have had time to tell him by now, I thought to myself, as I bounded out into the hall. And then I thought of something else and stopped.

"Mum?" I said, sticking my head back round the living room door. "Got any ice-cream in the fridge?"

"Yes – crunchy-nutty-toffee-something. Why?"

"I might need it – for medicinal purposes!"

By the puzzled looks my family gave me, I guess they might have thought that all the country air I'd been sniffing had made me go light-headed or something.

But I knew what I was doing. If that was Billy ringing the bell – like I suspected – then he'd probably have had some pretty lousy news by now.

And if that's the case, I thought, as I went to pull open the front door, *he'll need lots and lots of sympathy and a vat of ice-cream to get him through this...*

And that, Mum, is the whole story of my geography trip. No, I didn't learn very much about geography, but I learned something much more important ... that I deserve a Brownie Survival badge for surviving a week of the Clique, Feargal's wind-ups and Kyra's whiffy feet...

Love (and hugs and stuff)

Ally xoxoxoxoxoxox

PS Found a piece of squidged chocolate cake under my pillow this morning (blee!). A gift from Ivy, maybe? Rolf managed to eat it before I could pull the pillowcase off for washing.

PPS I know you were a bit worried about how gutted Billy seemed after being chucked by Sandie, but I think he's going to be OK (once his dented heart and bruised feelings get a chance to heal). Still, he's coming round for more moaning and sympathy today, and seeing as he got through all the ice-cream *and* a packet of Jaffa Cakes yesterday, I think it might be a good idea to hide the biscuit tin.

PPPS Can't wait for school on Monday – will Feargal go into hiding every time Kyra comes stomping along the corridor in her wedge sandals? Only if he has any sense (and that's debatable)...

Make sure you keep up with the gossip!

(14) HASSLES, HEART-PINGS! AND SAD, HAPPY ENDINGS...

Well, knock me down with a feather – just not one with superglue on (don't ask). The weirdness going on in my world means my head's even twistier than normal. First Sandie's parents break some big news, then Linn makes a scary announcement, and to top it all there's the, er, *heated* incident with Rowan and her Johnny Depp shrine. Nothing else could possibly surprise me ... not even if I opened the front door and found that I had a *boyfriend* on the doorstep... (Fat chance!)

Look out for loads more fab Ally's World books!

Find out more about Ally's World at

www.karenmccombie.com

brain full of plots, stupid stuff and cat hair
KMcC
the author

brain full of pictures, football and cat hair
the illustrator

WELCOME TO A WHOLE NEW WORLD...

STELLA ETC.

Find out who Stella is, meet her mad twin brothers, her best mate Frankie, and a mysterious fat ginger cat...

STELLA ETC. is Karen McCombie's super-cool new series – it's fab and it's coming soon!